A DUKE'S INTRODUCTION TO COURTSHIP

THE GENTLEMEN AUTHORS

SOPHIE BARNES

A DUKE'S INTRODUCTION TO COURTSHIP

The Gentlemen Authors

Cover Design by The Killion Group, Inc.

ALSO BY SOPHIE BARNES

Her Seafaring Scoundrel

More Than a Rogue

No Ordinary Duke

Secrets at Thorncliff Manor

Christmas at Thorncliff Manor

His Scandalous Kiss

The Earl's Complete Surrender

Lady Sarah's Sinful Desires

At The Kingsborough Ball

The Danger in Tempting an Earl

The Scandal in Kissing an Heir

The Trouble with Being a Duke

The Summersbys

The Secret Life of Lady Lucinda

There's Something About Lady Mary

Lady Alexandra's Excellent Adventure

Standalone Titles

The Girl Who Stepped Into The Past

How Miss Rutherford Got Her Groove Back

Novellas

Diamonds in the Rough

The Roguish Baron

The Enterprising Scoundrels

Mr. Clarke's Deepest Desire

Mr. Donahue's Total Surrender

The Townsbridges

An Unexpected Temptation

A Duke for Miss Townsbridge

Falling for Mr. Townsbridge

Lady Abigail's Perfect Match

When Love Leads To Scandal

Once Upon a Townsbridge Story

The Honorable Scoundrels

The Duke Who Came To Town

The Earl Who Loved Her

The Governess Who Captured His Heart

Standalone Titles

Only the Valet Will Do

Sealed with a Yuletide Kiss (An historical romance advent calendar)

The Secrets of Colchester Hall

Mistletoe Magic (from Five Golden Rings: A Christmas

Collection)

Miss Compton's Christmas Romance

CHAPTER ONE

London, August 1817

Brody Evans, Duke of Corwin, raised a celebratory glass of champagne. The atmosphere in his parlor was distinctly more buoyant today than it had been a few weeks earlier.

"A toast," he said, addressing his closest friends, Anthony Gibbs, the Duke of Westcliffe, and Callum Davis, the Duke of Stratton, as well as Anthony's new wife, Ada. "Congratulations, you two, on your recent marriage. And congratulations to us all for completing our novel."

"I still can't believe we got it done," Callum said after echoing Brody's congratulatory words regarding the wedding. He glanced at the thick stack of papers. Neatly assembled and tied with string, they'd been placed on a side table.

"All you need to do now is get it published," Ada said. She leaned toward Anthony and placed a tender kiss to his cheek. "I'm so incredibly proud of you. Of all of you. This is such a tremendous achievement, and the story is simply marvelous. I cannot wait for it to be released to the world."

Neither could Brody. Since coming to terms with his financial woes and discovering Anthony and Callum were in similar straits, they'd devised a solution together.

The idea to write a book had sprung to life when Anthony had entered the bookshop owned by Ada's uncle and discovered Ada shelving books. The pair had fallen into conversation with each other, and later into love. But the impact of their meeting on all three men was undeniable.

It had tested their creativity, resulting in a finished product they could be proud of. The hope was for the novel to sell well and make a decent profit – enough for them all to return to a state of financial security. Of course, other things had to be done as well. The book was not enough, considering the length of the process from idea to publication.

Anthony had already sold a couple of horses and some art work, his pianoforte, and a few other items in order to pay the servants and help support his wife and sisters. According to what he'd said earlier, a collection of Chinese vases were next on his list of things to get rid of.

Brody intended to follow suit. He could not blame all his financial woes on his younger brother, Finnegan, whose weakness for card play remained a problem. Brody knew he'd made his own mistakes too. Like Anthony and Callum, he'd squandered most of his fortune by trying to buy some happiness after his father's untimely death.

It hadn't worked.

If anything, it had only made matters worse, and now he realized how stupid he'd been. Granted, it did make it harder for him to admonish Finnegan for his reckless behavior, but the time had come for them both to be more responsible.

"I've made a list of prospective publishers," Anthony said. He set his glass aside and reached inside his jacket pocket to retrieve a piece of paper. "Considering the genre we've chosen, I thought we might approach Thomas Egerton and John Murray. Both published Miss Austen's novels, so I'm hopeful they will be willing to publish ours as well."

"Agreed," Brody said. When Anthony had initially suggested to him and Callum that they not only write a novel but that it should be a romance, he'd instinctively protested. But Anthony's reasoning had been sound. With Austen's recent death, there would be a gap in the market. Attempting to fill it and finding success would be easier than competing against the likes of Sir Walter Scott.

"Shall we pay them a visit tomorrow?" Callum asked.

Anthony nodded. "The sooner the better, I'd say."

"May I make a suggestion?" Brody asked. When everyone turned to him, he said, "Since none of us wants our name attached to this work, maybe Ada would be so kind as to represent us."

"As an agent of sorts?" she asked, tilting her head in question.

"I was thinking of you becoming the face of the author," Brody said. "It's simpler if the publisher thinks there's only one person to deal with instead of three. Plus, a woman would capture the essence of Miss Austen much better than three men. As such, the publisher might be more inclined to offer a deal."

"He makes a good point," Anthony said. "What do you think, Ada?"

"I suppose I could do it." Ada creased her brow for a moment. "I certainly don't mind as long as you're all in agreement, and you don't mind me taking the credit in public."

"Since public association with the novel is something we'd all like to avoid," Callum said, "I have no issue with this idea."

"Excellent." Brody grabbed the bottle of Veuve Clicquot and refilled all their glasses. "Another toast then, to the speedy success of *A Seductive Scandal*."

They clinked their glasses together and drank.

"I'll take this with me then," Ada said when she and Anthony were ready to leave. She collected the manuscript and hugged it against her breast as though it were the most precious thing in the world. "Anthony will send a note tomorrow evening to let you know how my meetings went. Hopefully, he'll have some good news to share."

Brody and Callum both thanked her.

"Do you think this endeavor will be as profitable as they expect?" Callum asked once Ada and Anthony had departed. He stood in Brody's foyer, preparing to head out as well.

Hands in pockets, Brody shrugged. "Let's hope so."

Callum took the hat and gloves Brody's butler, Rhys, handed him and waited until the man was gone before saying, "I've put most of the furniture at my country estate up for auction."

"I'm preparing to take similar measures," Brody assured him. "There's no other choice if I'm to keep running my London townhouse in the manner that's expected of a duke, although your solution does sound a bit drastic. Have things truly gotten that bad?"

"It's either that or deny Peter the chance to attend Eton. I've already booked his spot for next year and must pay for the first semester next month if he's to keep it."

Brody sympathized. While he had a troublesome younger brother to worry about, Callum was burdened by an even greater concern – namely that of being responsible for his cousin's only child. The boy's parents had both succumbed to a fever last year, and although they'd made some provisions for their son, it clearly wasn't enough for the sort of schooling with which Callum ought to provide the boy. He was a duke, after all. For his ward to attend anything less than Eton and later, Oxford or Cambridge, was unthinkable.

"I'm sorry," Brody said. "If there's anything I can do to help, please let me know."

"Thank you. I appreciate the offer, but you've your own problems to deal with." He put on his hat and reached for the door. "Let's just pray this book helps all three of us earn an income. Once we do that we can make some investments and get back to where we're meant to be."

"That is the plan," Brody agreed. He saw his friend out and shut the door, then returned to the parlor where a maid had already erased all traces of his friends' presence.

Turning, he surveyed the space. There was a long-case clock he liked but didn't really need since another clock stood on the fireplace mantle. A collection of porcelain figurines purchased by some long-lost relative might also fetch a decent price. And there was that ghastly Louis the Fourteenth cabinet he'd never liked. That alone should be worth at least forty pounds.

"Sorry to intrude," Rhys said when he came to find Brody later that afternoon. "There's a Mr. Apcot to see Lord Losturn."

Brody sighed. "I trust my brother has not yet risen?"

"He has not."

"And you're involving me because Mr. Apcot has suggested his business is unpleasant in nature?"

To his credit, Rhys maintained an inscrutable expression "No indication was required, Your Grace. The man is extremely blunt."

"I see."

"Would you rather I tell him no one's at home?" Rhys asked.

"No." Brody hated persistent problems and would rather get this one out of the way. "Please show him in."

The man who arrived in the parlor a few moments later was not the cutthroat type Brody had feared Finn might have gotten involved with, but a well-dressed gentleman with immaculate manners.

"Thank you for seeing me, Your Grace." Mr. Apcot declined Brody's invitation to sit and remained standing, so Brody did too. "I know you're a busy man, so I'll get to the point, shall I?"

"By all means." Brody clasped his hands behind his back and braced himself for impact.

"Lord Losturn owes me five hundred pounds – a sum I lent him nearly six months ago and which he has failed to repay."

Brody wasn't sure how he managed to maintain a calm demeanor when faced with such devastating information. Bloody hell. He gritted his teeth. "Go on."

"You are a duke. He is a marquess."

"An honorary one," Brody murmured.

"Nevertheless," Mr. Apcot said, his gaze sweeping the parlor as though with great deliberation. "You're not exactly paupers."

Looks could be deceiving, but essentially, Mr. Apcot was correct. They could get the funds one way or another. "I don't have the sum readily available, I'm afraid. Give me a month and—"

"You have one week. If I don't get my money by then, I'm afraid I'll have to resort to drastic measures."

Brody straightened his spine and took a step forward. "Is that a threat?"

"Much like you, I imagine, I've a reputation to consider."

Of course he did. Brody nodded. "One week it is."

He waited until Mr. Apcot was well and truly out the door before charging upstairs and thrusting open the door to Finnigan's bedchamber. Without pausing for breath, he crossed to the bed where his brother still slept.

"Get up." Brody tossed the blankets aside. "Right now."

Finnegan flung one arm over his head. "Go away."

"No." Brody grabbed his arm and gave it a yank.

"What the hell, Brody?"

"You have the gall to ask that of me after I've been called on by one of your moneylenders?" Brody muttered a curse. "Five hundred pounds is what Mr. Apcot insisted I give him. What in the name of Hades were you thinking?"

Finnegan groaned and squinted at Brody. "Can we please discuss this at a more reasonable hour?"

"It's almost five in the bloody afternoon. So no, we cannot."

"Fine." Finnegan pushed up into a sitting position and rubbed his eyes. An unhappy sigh followed. "You know how these games work and Mr. Apcot assured me I'd have a year to repay him."

As if that made it any better. "If that's true, then he's changed his mind. Which he is allowed to do unless you have a written contract of some sort."

"No one works out a contract while playing cards, Brody. You know that."

"Which makes your willingness to accept the funds Mr. Apcot offered to lend you all the more incredulous. Honestly, how reckless can you possibly be?"

Finnegan's eyes darkened. "Don't speak to me of

recklessness, Brody. You and I both know we wouldn't be in the financial straits we're in had it not been for your foolish spending."

It was the same argument as always, and one that was hard to dispute. Even so, Brody felt compelled to say, "Unlike you, I stopped spending when there was nothing left and am now attempting to make money rather than lose it. But these debts you keep acquiring aren't helping."

"I am aware. And I'm sorry." Finnegan climbed from the bed and padded across the floor to the washstand. "You know, I was only trying to help. I thought, if I could at least double the five hundred, we'd be all right for the next year."

Brody pinched the bridge of his nose. "While I appreciate that, gambling with money we do not have is a risky business. We're worse off now than we were before. Not to mention, this happened some six months ago and you failed to tell me. Had you done so, I might have found some way to prepare, but now…"

He sank into a chair that stood in one corner and tried to think of a viable solution.

"How much do we have in the bank?"

A miserable laugh rolled up Brody's throat. "Roughly twenty pounds, most of which will have to go toward paying the taxes and our servants."

"How about that project you mentioned?"

Finnegan washed his face and reached for a towel. "A novel, I think you said?"

"We have to sell it to a publisher first. If we're lucky, we'll get an advance, but what if we don't? Printing is bound to take time, so in my estimation we're looking at a few months before there's a hope of making a steady income from that." Leaning forward, he braced his forearms on his thighs and stared at the floor. "I've considered a few other options for the immediate future, but implementing them within one week will be close to impossible."

Finnegan rang the bell-pull and waited for the valet they shared to arrive. "One of us could marry. I hear Viscount Ebberly's daughter, Miss Starling, has an impressive dowry so maybe—"

Brody's gaze snapped to his brother's. "Stay away from that woman, Finn. She's nothing but trouble – almost wrecked Westcliffe's life with her selfish deceit."

"But—"

"If she becomes my sister-in-law," Brody warned while rising from the chair, "you and I are through. Is that understood?"

"Right. Got it."

"Good."

Their valet, Jackson, arrived at that moment, putting a natural end to their conversation. Brody turned for the door only to tell his brother succinctly, "Don't leave the house. Stay home. We'll continue this conversation later. Over dinner."

Meanwhile, he had an errand to run – one he'd been putting off much too long. He called for the carriage to be brought round – another comfort he probably ought to get rid of. With most of his time spent in London, he could easily use the hackneys when traveling longer distances. But what sort of duke would he be without a carriage bearing his crest?

He climbed inside as soon as it pulled up in front of the house and instructed the driver to take him to The Strand. Settling against the squabs, he pondered the pointlessness of the show he was forced to put on because of a title. A title that was proving to be incredibly inconvenient.

Were he a mere mister, he could get by with a maid of all works and a house one tenth the size of the one he currently lived in. He'd not have a country estate to manage either. Or be expected to host at least one ball a year.

He shook his head as the horse clip-clopped at an easy gait through the dimming afternoon light. If those less fortunate heard him complain they'd think him ungrateful, but the fact was that having multiple homes and all the expenses that came along with them was lovely when one was wealthy. If one was close to ruination, however, it was something else entirely – a burden that seemed to get heavier every day.

The carriage pulled to a gentle halt outside a handsome townhouse where window boxes were filled with a pretty selection of pink roses. Brody waited for his accompanying footman to open the door before climbing down onto the pavement. He paused there briefly then strode to the door.

Three solid raps ensured his call was answered by Barlow, the man Brody had hired to serve as Florence's butler.

"You'll find her in the music room," Barlow said after taking Brody's hat and gloves. "Would you like me to ask for some tea to be brought up?"

"No. Thank you. That won't be necessary. I don't intend to stay long."

If this surprised Barlow, as it ought, he gave no indication of it. Instead, he merely inclined his head and made himself scarce. Brody took a deep breath, reminded himself of his reason for coming, and went in search of his mistress.

He found her at the pianoforte, playing a jolly tune that stood in stark contrast to his mood. Attempting a smile to dampen the blow he would soon deliver, he moved into her line of vision.

"Corwin!" She abandoned the music and came to greet him.

She lifted her mouth to his, kissing him with the same sort of hunger he'd always found so wonderfully distracting. It had little effect today, but he kissed her back anyway, for old time's sake.

At four and twenty years of age, with long curly hair and a voluptuous figure, she'd been his mistress for nearly three years. Ever since he'd first seen her perform at the Haymarket Theatre.

"I wasn't expecting you until Friday," she said, pressing herself against him with what could only be described as keen interest. "Shall we head upstairs?"

"No. My visit today will be brief."

She leaned back a little, her soulful eyes meeting his. "Oh?"

There was no easy way about this. Best get it done with as swiftly as possible. "I'm sorry, but I've come to inform you that our acquaintance must come to an end."

"I don't understand." Her gaze searched his. "Are you to be married?"

He shook his head. "No."

"The last time we met you spoke of how much you enjoyed my company. You said you appreciated my friendship and the confidences I've kept on your behalf."

"Confidences which ought to explain my reasoning, Florence. You've known my situation for a while now. If you'll recall, I warned you it might come to this, though I do regret the suddenness." Each word he uttered tasted bitter, but what else was he to do? "I'm afraid I can't afford to keep you any longer. As it stands, I see no recourse but to sell this house and let the servants go."

She raised her chin even as her eyes welled with tears. "It's all right. Margate approached me a few weeks ago. I'll see if he still has an interest."

"If not, please let me know." She pulled away and he released her, watching as she went to stare out the window. "My financial situation might have gone to hell, but I'm still well connected. I'm happy to introduce you to my gentlemen friends."

"Thank you." She was silent a moment before she asked, "How long do I have?"

"One week."

She whipped back around. "You cannot expect me to move out in such a short time, Corwin. It's unreasonable."

"I know, and I'm sorry, but there's an issue forcing my hand – a situation that must be dealt with – and this is the only solution available to me on such short notice." He'd put the house on the market at once. If he could at least get an offer with a down payment, he'd be able to deal with Mr. Apcot.

Florence shook her head. "You're serious?"

"Unfortunately so." How he wished he could give her more time.

She didn't respond but merely stood there, glaring at him through watery eyes. He wondered if she knew how effective it was. His gut twisted, even though this wasn't his fault. It was Finn's, though his loyalty toward his brother prevented him from saying as much. So he repeated his promise to help her move on, should she need it, and wished her well before going to speak with Barlow. The butler would have to stop by with the key once the house had been vacated.

Until then, a well-placed advertisement in *The Mayfair Chronicle* would hopefully help take the house off his hands.

CHAPTER TWO

The note that arrived for Brody the following afternoon did not improve his mood.

Dear Duke of Corwin,

My meetings with Egerton and Murray were unproductive. Neither publisher claimed an interest in the novel. I've met with a third – Rowe & Sons – but they said I'd have to wait a month to get an answer, and I refused to leave the manuscript with them that long. I'll set up other appointments in the coming days and shall keep you informed on my progress.

Sincerely,

Ada Westcliffe

Blast!

Brody poured himself a glass of brandy and tossed back the contents. If the book didn't sell, they'd all have wasted precious time that might have been better spent on other pursuits. What those pursuits might have been, he'd no idea, but he was sure he'd have come up with something if he hadn't been focused on writing a novel.

Disheartened by his situation as a whole, he expelled a deep breath and sank against his chair. If only his father were still alive, then none of this would have happened. But losing him had been much like having a limb cut off. His life had been forever changed from one day to the next.

God, how he missed him. Even now, three years later, he still expected to see him walk through the door.

Brody swept one hand across his brow. It was hard to grasp the unfairness of it. Papa and his friends had all been perfectly healthy. They'd been having a brilliant time, visiting a farm to buy some livestock. Who could have predicted the explosion that would take place in that cow pen? To this day, Brody had no idea how it had happened. What he did know was that his father had been struck in the head by a beam when the roof had collapsed. It wasn't even the explosion itself that had killed him.

He snatched up his glass and prepared to refill it, only to stop himself at the last second. What was he doing? Getting foxed wasn't the answer.

Setting the glass aside, he left his study and went to collect his hat and gloves. A brisk walk to clear his head was what he required. Leaving the house, he took a deep lungful of warm London air and set his course for Oxford Street. An overcast sky suggested a light rain later, but for now, it was comfortably dry.

He tipped his hat to a couple of ladies coming the opposite way. They smiled in return and wished him a pleasant day. He echoed their greeting and kept walking to avoid getting caught up in meaningless conversation. What he needed was to figure out how to deal with Finn. Their dinner together last night had been unproductive, and although Finn had sworn he wouldn't make matters worse, Brody worried his brother might not be able to stop himself.

Gambling could be a terrible addiction. Brody had heard of men resorting to drastic measures because of the hold it had upon them. Some had stolen the money they owed while other poor souls had taken their lives to escape debtor's prison. Brody shuddered at the idea of such a fate befalling the brother he'd always loved so dearly. Somehow, they had to get through this. Preferably without Mama finding out.

He groaned. How many times had she warned him to be more careful with his spending? Not only had he refused to listen, he'd also failed to keep his brother in check. If she found out how bad things had gotten, he'd never hear the end of it.

The only option right now—make sure the townhouse where Florence had lived sold, even if it went for less than what it was worth.

His feet kept moving, taking him through the hustle and bustle of increased traffic until he reached the spot where Bond Street began. This was where he did most of his shopping. He'd soon reach his favorite tailor, the cobbler where his father had taken him for his sixteenth birthday, and the milliner where he purchased his hats.

These were not the low-end shops one might find in the East End, but exclusive boutiques with custom made goods fashioned according to the highest standard. Expensive was another way of putting it.

Shoving his hands in his pockets, he continued past the shops to where Bond Street spilled onto Piccadilly. An intersection forced him to slow his pace briefly to allow for a draught horse and cart to pass. A newspaper boy on the corner ahead called out the news of the day – a scandalous kiss at a soiree, another debutante ruined.

Brody snorted and kept walking. Crates were being unloaded and carried into a nearby winery while the tea shop next door was beginning to bustle with afternoon guests. A few drops of water landed on him as he walked past the tobacconist on the next corner. He stopped and considered returning home before the rain began in earnest.

But as he turned and his gaze swept along the

length of the side street, he spotted a sign. Hudson & Co. Publishing. Intrigued, he approached the business which was constructed from red brick and had tall glass windows framed in dark green. He stopped for a closer look and noted the five men crammed inside the small office. Bundles of paper tied with twine littered the floor while additional ones were placed on each desk.

An older portly fellow reclined in his chair while flipping through pages, licking his fingers between each one. He grabbed a pencil from behind his ear and made a quick note before looking toward the window. His gaze caught Brody's and held for a second before he gestured toward a spot located to Brody's left. Brody's attention shifted toward the notice stuck on the door.

Assistant Editor Required. All interested parties may apply.

He almost laughed. Was the man suggesting he seek employment? Him? A duke?

Additional raindrops warned him of an impending drizzle. He shook his head and prepared to head for home when several thoughts struck all at once. He and his friends needed a publisher. He also needed money. Was working truly beneath him if it helped acquire a publishing deal and provided him with some extra coin?

Perhaps one day in the future, when he'd dug himself out of the mess he and Finn had created, he could be pickier. But right now, securing this position before someone else did made sense. It would provide him with access. Hell, he could pitch his own book and approve it.

With a quick backward glance, just to be sure no one of his acquaintance saw him, Brody pulled the door open and hurried inside. His elbow connected with something or someone blocking his path. A soft grunt followed and Brody lowered his gaze to the young man who'd been coming the opposite way. With the notice on the door window and the lad's inferior height, Brody hadn't seen him until it was too late.

A bewildered expression was accompanied by a frown as the lad stared up at him from beneath the brim of a brown woolen cap.

"You," he said, then sucked in a breath, swallowed hard, and pushed past Brody with a muttered, "excuse me."

Brody blinked in rapid succession and turned just in time to glimpse the lad's back as he left the building. The door swung shut behind him. Brody knit his brow, certain he'd seen that face somewhere before, though he could not think of where.

"May I help you?" asked the fellow who'd made him aware of the job opening.

Brody gave up trying to place the lad and turned to the man. "I'd like to inquire about the position."

"Excellent." The man wiped his hand on his

trousers and extended it to Brody. "I'm Mr. Hudson, owner of this here enterprise."

Inhaling deeply, Brody accepted the handshake. "Mr. Evans, aspiring editor."

Mr. Hudson grinned and rocked back on his heels. "Come on. Let's have a chat in the office."

Brody was led toward Mr. Hudson's desk, which stood amid four others. An extra chair was acquired so Brody could sit. He did so at the same time as Mr. Hudson, making sure to keep his face averted from the widow, lest he be discovered by someone he knew.

"Tell me about your schooling," said Mr. Hudson.

"Um…" Brody wasn't sure he ought to mention his private tutor, Eton, or Oxford. He finally settled on, "It was thorough."

"So you can read and write?"

Brody gaped at him. Surely his attire spoke for itself. "Of course."

"Just making sure since the job does require such skill."

Brody sent him a tight smile. "How much does it pay?"

"Six shillings a week."

It was hard to hide the extent of his disappointment. Six shillings was barely more than what his downstairs maid received. He'd hoped this job would earn him a lot more and had to remind himself of its added benefit.

"And what precisely does the position entail?"

"You'll be reading. Pick a pile, start at the top, and work your way through it. If an opening sentence grabs you, read the paragraph. If you're still hooked, keep reading until you lose interest. If you don't by the time you've reached the third chapter, recommend the story to me. That's it."

"Will you provide me with an indication of what you might be looking for?"

"The next bestselling author. Plain and simple." Mr. Hudson drummed his fingers on his armrest. "Well?"

Brody glanced around and decided there were worse things in life than having to sit in a room with five other men and read. Especially since he had nothing better to do with his time. And if the job led to a publishing contract, it would be worth every second.

If not, he could always quit.

"I accept," he told Mr. Hudson. "When do I start?"

"At once," Mr. Hudson informed him. He showed Brody to a small desk in the far corner of the room and gestured toward the manuscripts stacked in various piles. "Start reading and let me know if you think you've struck gold."

CHAPTER THREE

Harriet Michaels rushed around the street corner before stopping to catch her breath. Her heart raced faster than a curricle bound for Gretna Greene. It was him. The same man who'd bumped into her last week on her way to work.

Her pace had been brisk that morning, her thoughts on the bright and happy future she hoped to ensure for her younger sister, Lucy. She'd turned onto Holborn and—oomph. The handsomest man she'd ever laid eyes on ploughed straight into her.

The very man who'd just entered her place of employment, knocking her sideways once more and turning her world upside down.

With one hand braced against the brick siding, she closed her eyes briefly and focused on getting her nerves to stop hopping about in her stomach.

What was he doing here?

Not looking for her. That much was clear. The lack of recognition she'd seen on his face suggested that colliding with others was such a common occurrence for him, he paid no attention to whom he collided with. She huffed a breath. Just as well since having others take note of her wasn't in her best interest.

With her red curls cropped in a masculine style and the clothes she elected to wear, she'd managed to hide her sex, and in so doing had acquired a job that not only earned her a decent wage but that she also enjoyed. A rarity, for people in her position. But she'd worked hard, proven herself, and was well enough educated to outperform anyone else looking for similar work.

And with a twelve-year-old sister to care for, it was imperative she kept her head down, avoided attracting attention, and prevented her employer from figuring out she was a woman. He'd most likely sack her on the spot if he knew. Not only because she'd deceived him, but because the business she dealt in had been reserved for men.

Pushing away from the wall, she recommenced walking. The errand she had to run, collecting the recently ordered title block for a novel they'd start printing tomorrow, would hopefully distract her from those sky-blue eyes. A task she'd found unreasonably difficult to accomplish since her first encounter with whomever the gentleman happened to be.

She'd no idea and she did not care.

Not exactly true.

But she *should* not care, so she wouldn't. Instead she would focus on her task, the wages she'd be receiving next week when the month drew to a close, and making sure her sister, Lucy, was properly fed and their rented room paid for on time.

That was what mattered. Not some incredibly tall and strikingly handsome man who somehow managed to make her forget time and place every time their paths crossed. Probably because he'd physically jolted her on both occasions. It was hard to keep one's thoughts in order when one was being jostled about.

It certainly had nothing to do with the subtle smile he'd given her with his full lips or the warmth in his eyes when his gaze had met hers. She'd barely noticed his blonde hair curling from under the brim of his hat or the fact that his shoulders were almost as wide as the door.

Nor had it occurred to her that his clothes weren't as flashy as they'd been the first time she'd seen him several days ago. She definitely did not wonder if he might have been on his way home from some fancy event on that particular morning.

No. She'd barely given the man any thought, she

decided as she reached her destination. There was certainly little point in doing so since he would likely be gone from her place of employment by the time she returned. Which did make her wonder about his reason for visiting Hudson & Co. in the first place.

No matter.

It wasn't any business of hers.

Satisfied that she'd concluded her musings where Mr. Anonymous was concerned, she returned to Hudson & Co. an hour later, entering through the back door since this took her straight to the printing room.

"I've got the title block," she informed her colleagues, James, Matthew, and Oliver. James and Matthew took turns inking the type and providing the strength required to work the lever on the letter-press. Meanwhile, Oliver read the manuscript so she could set the type quicker. "Let's finish *The Collapse of the Roman Empire* now so we can get ahead of schedule and start on *Scottish Wildflowers* tomorrow.

"That'll involve working late." James leaned against a heavy wood table and crossed his legs at the ankles while sending her a steady look from behind a pair of serious eyes.

"Possibly, but wouldn't you rather do that and try to earn a bonus than risk having your wages cut when Mr. Hudson decides we're not efficient enough?"

"I could do with the extra blunt myself," Matthew

said. With his hands shoved into his grey trouser pockets, he punctuated the statement by spitting into a bin that stood on the floor.

"Same here," said Oliver.

Turning to James, Harriet raised an eyebrow. "Well?"

He hesitated a moment, then muttered a curse. "Fine."

"Let's get started right away then." Harriet set the parcel she'd collected on a shelf, then removed her jacket and hung it on a wall hook. Rolling up her sleeves, she crossed to the wide wall unit filled with drawers where she spent the most time. A shelf was set in the middle so she could collect the compositing sticks she needed and set them there while assembling the sorts—letters and punctuation marks.

Oliver perched himself on a nearby stool and picked up the manuscript. He read the next sentence and Harriet collected the sorts she required without having to check the labels on the drawers. She filled a series of compositing sticks, placed them in type galleys and transferred these to forms that would be used to create the page layouts. They were then set aside for James to collect so Matthew could ink them.

Her speed had improved tremendously during the time she'd worked here. When James had timed her last, she'd achieved an astonishing one thousand five hundred sorts per hour, which was one hundred more than what was considered the highest standard within the industry.

"We're ready for the next form," Matthew shouted, and Harriet swiftly added the punctuation mark she needed, placed the last compositing stick in the type galley, arranged the galleys in a form, and gave it to James when he appeared at her shoulder.

"Read faster," Harriet told Oliver. They'd managed to get their momentum going. The papers were flying onto the press, the sorts she prepared getting inked and printed with admirable speed.

She swiped her brow and grabbed a new compositing stick. The heat in the room increased, causing sweat to gather at the nape of her neck and across her back. The smell of chemicals rolled up her nose, and she paused for a second to open another window up under the ceiling so more air could enter.

Behind her, James lowered the platen on the press, causing the familiar groan of machinery to fill the room. Harriet slid another completed form to the edge of her table and went to work on the next compositing stick while Oliver kept on reading.

"One more page and we're done," Oliver told everyone a couple of hours later.

Although she couldn't relax yet, Harriet breathed a welcome sigh of relief. They were almost finished. "Time?"

"Nearing seven," Matthew shouted.

Good. They'd be done a bit sooner than she'd expected. She prepared the last forms and handed them over, then sagged against the cabinet and allowed herself to savor their accomplishment. "Great job everyone."

"You were right to press us," James said as he cleaned up later. "It's nice having this over and done with so we can begin the new project tomorrow."

"Mr. Hudson will be pleased," Matthew said.

"Let's hope so," Harriet said.

"Anyone up for a celebratory drink at the tavern around the corner?" Oliver asked, putting on his hat.

"I really ought to get home to my wife," James said. "Some other time perhaps."

"How about you two?" Oliver asked once James had left.

"I'll join you," Matthew said.

"And you, Harry?" Oliver sent her a hopeful look.

She shook her head. "Sorry. I've got to get home."

"Why the rush?" Matthew asked. "You don't have a wife waiting for you with a rolling pin the way James does. Unlucky bastard. I never understood why he married that woman."

Harriet grabbed her cap and shoved it down over her head. "I've got a sister though. You know that."

"Right. Of course." Matthew's expression brightened. "You should bring her along. Introduce her to us."

"Not on your life," Harriet told him. "She's only twelve years old and even if she weren't, I'd not let a roguish scoundrel like you within fifty yards of her, Matthew."

Matthew grinned. "You can't blame a man for trying."

"Trying what?" Oliver asked. "You've made your position as a permanent bachelor clear."

"I could be persuaded to change that stance, I suspect. If I met the right woman." He slapped Harry on the back. "Too bad they're not like us men in the way they think and behave. We're logical creatures, right? Women though…" He shook his head and gave a low whistle. "Nothing but flights of fancy and high expectations."

Harriet wasted no time in voicing her agreement. "Quite so, which is why I believe it's best to avoid the parson's mousetrap."

"While getting whatever one needs from a Coventry nun," Oliver said with a grin.

Harriet had no idea what that might be, but managed to work it out when Matthew said, "You'd do well to avoid them like the plague unless you're looking to get a lot more for your money than pleasure. Better visit a clean establishment instead, like Amourette's. You'll find it on Parker's Lane. The women there get regular checkups to make sure they don't pose a danger to their clients."

It took a bit of effort for Harriet not to stare at

Matthew in shock and to remember that he thought she was one of the lads with whom he could speak of this sort of thing freely. Still, the very idea of paying someone for that sort of thing made her skin itch. To say nothing of the poor women who had no choice but to lower themselves to such an unseemly profession.

Thank goodness she'd thought to disguise herself and that the disguise had proven effective. Otherwise, she too ran the risk of being taken advantage of since lower-class women could easily fall prey to cruel men. Especially if they were pretty. Not that she was either of those things. Her family was gentry, but life had been both unfair and hard after the death of her father.

She shook herself free from that thought and, realizing Matthew and Oliver watched her, quickly nodded. "I quite agree. The last thing anyone wants is the pox."

"Hear, hear," Matthew said while Oliver directed a curious look at Harriet that made her feel more than a little uneasy. She hoped he'd not seen through her disguise.

But then he nodded and suggested he and Matthew head off.

"I'll lock up," she informed the pair. There was one more thing she wanted to do before leaving, and that was check the manuscript they would start on in the morning. If she could also prepare the sorts for the first two forms, she'd be especially pleased. It shouldn't take long.

Oliver and Matthew wished her good night and headed off. The door slammed behind them and Harriet grabbed the bundle of papers that constituted *Scottish Wildflowers*. She set it on the work table and cut the twine it was tied with, using a knife. Besides the title block she'd collected, several compositing sticks would have to be prepared for the author name, publishing house, and publication date. After that, came the introduction – a one page tightly penned piece.

Harriet collected a new compositing stick and began placing the sorts. It took a bit longer without Oliver's help since she had to stop and read all the time, but getting it done would lead to an easier start in the morning.

She expelled a satisfied breath once she'd finished and glanced at the clock that sat on a nearby shelf. It was almost half past eight. Time for her to get back to Lucy and make sure she ate something decent. She picked up two of the forms she'd prepared and carried them to the inking table where James was most likely to see them if he arrived before she did tomorrow.

But as she passed the door that led to the front of the building where Mr. Hudson and his editors worked, it flew open, straight into Harriet. The impact knocked several sorts loose and sent them flying.

"For bloody crying out loud," she exclaimed, then blinked a few times when she saw who had entered the room. She stared at him. Surely this had to be some sort of joke. "What are you doing here?"

The stranger who kept walking into her gave her a blank look. "Mr. Hudson employed me."

She groaned in frustration. *Brilliant.* Her attempt at forgetting all about him and his inadvertent ability to sweep her off her feet at every opportunity had been made impossible by the very fact that they were now colleagues.

To make matters worse, heat was creeping into her cheeks.

Hoping to hide it, she knelt to gather the pieces of sort that were scattered across the floor. It was all very odd. Although he was modestly dressed today, he'd looked like an upper-class gentleman when she'd last seen him. Not like someone in need of employment.

"I'm terribly sorry," he said as he dropped to a crouch and proceeded to help clean the mess.

"Might I suggest you look where you're going in future?" She kept her attention firmly on the floor, refusing to look at him even though his voice alone made her shiver with pleasure.

Good grief. Shiver with pleasure? From no more

than a voice? Whoever had heard of such nonsense before?

"My apologies once again."

"This is the third time you've bumped into me within the course of one week." She snatched up a sort and returned it to the correct compositing stick. "If I didn't know any better I'd think it deliberate."

He chuckled in a manner that only annoyed her further because of how utterly charming she found it. Gah! It was imperative she get away soon. Before she glanced at him without thinking and lost all common sense.

"Your face did strike me as familiar when I arrived this afternoon, though I can't for the life of me figure out why."

She collected a few more pieces which she proceeded to jam back into place. "You knocked into me last week while walking along Holborn."

"That was you?" He sounded amused. "While I do recall the incident, I would never have recognized you. In fact, I'm surprised you recognized me."

"And why is that?" she asked, reaching for a sort that had landed next to his foot.

He went for it at the same time, his fingers connecting with hers instead of the small piece of type. Jerking back, he cleared his throat while she sucked in a breath and tried to remain as still as she could. She couldn't afford to reveal the shocking effect his touch had evoked.

"Sorry," he muttered. "Didn't mean to do that."

"It's fine," she lied. The lingering sparks still pricked at her skin. This was possibly the furthest from 'fine' she'd ever been. This man was wreaking havoc not only upon her mind but on her body as well. It was intolerable.

She grabbed the last two sorts and stood.

"Anyway," said Mr. Clumsy, "in answer to your previous question, I merely think it curious for a man to pay excessive attention to what another man looks like. They're just random passersby on the street."

Harriet winced. How stupid she'd been to reveal she'd taken notice of his appearance – that she recognized him after no more than a one split second glimpse. He'd turned away that day and continued on his way while she'd been left rather flummoxed, staring after him while attempting to calm her leaping pulse.

"Your boots," she blurted, sounding like a cretin.

Her ears burned. She wanted to smack herself. Instead she swallowed past the sudden dryness in her throat and forced herself to look directly at him. It wasn't easy since it was much like staring straight at the sun. Nevertheless, she did it, even though she could feel herself flushing, the heat not confined to her face but spreading rapidly down her neck and across her shoulders.

Still, she was fairly certain she managed to give

him the most acerbic expression possible when all he did was blink in return.

"They were the finest I've ever seen," she explained.

He frowned. "I don't see how that helped your recognition of me since I'm wearing shoes today."

"Right." *Pull yourself together, you nitwit.* She raised her chin just enough to convey the sort of confidence she required in this instance. "They simply compelled me to take notice. Of you, that is. And besides, I'm quite good with faces. Once I've seen one, it tends to stick."

"Hmm…" He angled his head. "You ought to work for Bow Street."

She ought to get her head examined. Deciding a smile would be her safest response that was what she resorted to.

The man blinked again then shook his head and extended his hand. "Mr. Evans. I'm the new assistant editor."

"Harry Michaels. Compositor." She took the hand he offered while steeling herself against the effect she feared the contact would have. A wise decision, she decided one second later when his long fingers closed around hers. It felt as though she'd been struck by lightning.

How she kept her footing and managed not to gasp was beyond her. What she did notice was that his eyes widened a fraction as though he'd felt it too.

Which was something she imagined he must find rather distressing.

If so, he gave no indication of it. He merely smiled, tightened his grip, and gave her hand a solid shake before releasing it altogether.

"A pleasure to make your acquaintance." He glanced past her shoulder. "Mr. Hudson sent me to find a title block for *Scottish Wildflowers*. He said to look for it here."

"Mr. Hudson hasn't departed yet?" Harriet was surprised. Her employer usually left a bit earlier in the day.

"He and I started chatting after work." Mr. Evans shrugged as though that explained everything.

"Right." Harriet turned and went to collect the title block. "This is what he asked for."

"Great. Thank you. And once again, I'm sorry about bumping into you. Won't happen again."

It was odd, how disappointed that made her feel. She gave a quick nod and said nothing further, watching instead as he left the room, shutting the door as he did so.

Only then, once he was gone, did reality fully sink in.

He, the man who made her heart leap with nary a glance, worked here now. She would see him every day. On a regular basis.

She stared at the door through which he'd departed and wondered how she'd survive the danger he posed not only to her livelihood but to her life. If anyone ever became suspicious of her inclination for him, her only way to avoid a hanging would be to reveal her true self. And risk losing the job she prized so dearly.

CHAPTER FOUR

"Have a good evening," Brody told Mr. Hudson as they parted ways around nine. He'd longed to return home earlier, but instinct had stopped him. If he was to earn Mr. Hudson's respect and make the man listen to him when he pitched the book he wanted to print, he had to prove himself worthy and gain his trust.

Part of this involved working hard enough to impress him. Beyond that, Brody had decided to put in the effort required to get to know the man. Friendship, of a sort, could be extremely beneficial. So he'd asked Mr. Hudson a few leading questions about Hudson & Co., how he'd started it and what he believed the future of printing might look like.

Thankfully, the publisher was happy to talk. And to be honest, Brody had found the information compelling. The history of printing in general had fascinated him, and Mr. Hudson's story-telling abilities were captivating. Three hours had flown by with no trouble at all.

In fact, he actually looked forward to meeting for work again the next day and helping Mr. Hudson increase his earnings by finding the sort of best-selling novel he sought.

Happy with his decision to take the job, he started his homeward trek. None of the manuscripts he'd read today had captured his interest, but this was, according to what he'd been told, to be expected.

Another interesting point in the day had been meeting Mr. Michaels. Funny that, how life sometimes worked. Who'd have thought he'd run into the same lad he'd bumped into once on the street?

Mr. Michaels probably thought him an oaf with two left feet, knocking into everyone in his path. He smiled despite his embarrassment over the situation since it was, if not funny, per se, then at least somewhat farcical. Though he wasn't sure Mr. Michaels saw it that way. He'd seemed rather put out by Brody's clumsiness. And who could blame him?

Brody had not just banged the door into the young man's shoulder and made him stumble but had caused him to spill two tray-like items with all of those neatly arranged letters in them. A lot of hard work gone to waste.

Brody took a deep breath and expelled it. Some

of those letters were very tiny. He couldn't imagine the skill it required to line them up snuggly against one another. And it had to be done fast too, according to what Mr. Hudson had told him.

The man had actually praised Mr. Michaels as one of the best compositors he'd ever known, remarking that his slim and delicate fingers were likely to blame. Brody had noticed those fingers when he and Mr. Michaels had cleaned up the spill. He'd noticed a great many things. Too many, for his peace of mind.

Quickening his pace, he crossed the street behind a passing carriage and stepped onto the pavement. He turned left, the heels of his shoes clicking loudly against the stone tiles. A man should not consider the length of another man's eyelashes or the delicate nature of his jawline. He definitely shouldn't feel a response to his touch, besides a brotherly connection if one were close friends.

Brody wasn't the least bit close to Mr. Michaels. They'd only just met. So the flash of heat he'd experienced when their fingers touched the first time and the leap of his pulse when they'd shaken hands alarmed him a little.

Although, to be fair, Mr. Michaels was unusually petite for a man. Physically, he was more of a boy really, but age-wise, he looked like he was at least eighteen. Which was probably what had caught his attention. As for the heat, it had been quite warm in that room, and his increased heart rate could be due to how foolish he'd felt in the moment. Generally speaking.

He was a duke for heaven's sake. Yet rather than come across with the sense of authority he was used to exerting, he'd appeared a bumbling idiot.

Tomorrow he'd have to do better, he decided. No more rushing about. He'd take care when rounding a corner or entering a room, to be sure Mr. Michaels wouldn't be in his path. And then he'd ask the fellow if he'd like to go for a drink after work. That ought to smooth things over.

Satisfied, and not the least bit concerned over why Mr. Michaels's opinion mattered so greatly, Brody returned home to find an anxious Rhys waiting.

"Thank goodness you're well," said the butler. He took Brody's hat and gloves and set them aside. "I was preparing to call Bow Street."

"Whatever for?"

"Because it's almost ten o'clock." Rhys said this as though no additional explanation were required. When Brody merely stared at him, Rhys added, "You always eat dinner at home at precisely seven o'clock."

"Oh dear." Brody had been so caught up in his new sense of purpose, he'd forgotten everything else. "I'm terribly sorry. Is Cook very angry with me?"

"She was, but I think she'll be fine by morning when she finds out you haven't been murdered.

Truth is, we were all quite worried, your brother included."

"Forgive me, Rhys, but something came up – a project of sorts – so I do believe keeping late hours will be the norm for some time. You mentioned my brother. Is Losturn at home?"

"He is indeed, Your Grace."

Brody was not just surprised. He was extremely pleased. "Excellent. I'll have a word with him then."

"Very good, Your Grace. He's in your study."

"Perfect."

Brody turned, prepared to head in that direction when Rhys quietly told him, "I'm happy to know all is well."

It wasn't yet, but Brody had no intention of bringing that up with his butler. So he merely dipped his head and offered his thanks before continuing on his way. Tomorrow morning, he'd dispatch notes to Anthony and Callum, informing them that he too was working on getting their novel published.

In case Ada's efforts failed.

CHAPTER FIVE

Despite expecting to see Mr. Evans the following day when she returned to work, Harriet managed to avoid him by choosing to arrive through the back entrance. And since Oliver was happy to fetch the title block they needed from Mr. Hudson, she had no reason to enter the front office where Mr. Evans would likely be found.

Still, she remained forever conscious of his presence in the building, constantly on alert and freezing up slightly whenever the door to the print room opened.

"Is everything all right?" Oliver asked when they closed for the day. "You've been looking over your shoulder a lot today, like you keep expecting someone to sneak up on you."

"It's nothing." She grabbed her things and

followed him to the door, exiting after James and Matthew. "Felt a bit drafty, that's all."

"Hmm…" Oliver frowned but didn't address the issue further, choosing instead to say, "I met the new assistant editor when I went to collect the title block. Pleasant fellow. Have you seen him yet?"

Harriet closed the door and locked it with the key Mr. Hudson had given her when he'd increased her pay a couple of months ago. She turned to face her three colleagues. "He came to the print room yesterday after you'd left. Knocked the door straight into me."

"And?" Oliver asked. "What was your impression?"

"Besides being clumsy?" Harriet shrugged, doing her best to feign indifference. "I suppose I'd consider him to be polite. He apologized numerous times for the blunder. Besides that, I really can't say."

"Why are we even discussing him?" James inquired. "It's not like we'll be working with him."

"Exactly," said Matthew. He lit a cheroot, took a long drag and offered it to Harriet, who turned down the offer. Matthew passed it to James instead. "The editors don't associate with us lot. Different class of people, aren't they?"

"Not vastly so," Oliver argued. "I pretty much do the same as them, sitting about and reading all day."

"The rest of us don't." Matthew took the cheroot

from James and set it to his lips for a slow inhale. A cloud of smoke was exhaled moments later. "We supply the muscle, which makes us no different than laborers. Not that I'm complaining. I prefer being physically active, and Mr. Hudson's a good employer."

"But we don't mingle. Do we, Harry?"

Harriet met James's gaze. "No."

"Fine by me," Oliver said. He slung the strap from the satchel he carried to work every day across his shoulder. "Mind if I walk with you, Harry? I'm heading to my sister's and if memory serves, she doesn't live far from you."

"All right," Harriet said, appreciating the company. They parted ways with James and Matthew, who were headed in the opposite direction, and proceeded toward Piccadilly.

"I didn't want to ask while the others were around," Oliver said after several moments of silence, "but I was wondering if you might want to grab a drink with me one evening."

"Just the two of us?" Harriet asked, to be perfectly clear.

"Yeah. I mean, I don't know if you realize, but I consider you to be my best mate. Thought it might be fun to spend some more time together. Outside of work."

"Oh." She dodged a couple of men who were coming in the opposite direction. As soon as she'd passed them and Oliver had fallen into step beside her once more, she told him, "I'm afraid it might be difficult for me to do so. As you know, I've got Lucy to tend to."

"My sister has already said she'd be happy to watch her for you. And it doesn't have to be more than a couple of hours."

His eagerness and the fact that he'd already started planning for it put Harriet on edge. She glanced at him and wondered once more if he might have realized she wasn't male after all. Probably not, or he would have said something now while they were alone. Wouldn't he?

She shook her head. Oliver was a likeable man, easy to talk to, helpful and considerate. Working with him was a pleasure since he consistently seemed to be one step ahead of her, always aware of what she needed and when. If he truly believed her to be his best mate, she ought to be flattered, not suspicious.

"I'll have to think about it," she said, deliberately stalling for time. Considering the position she was in, it was imperative she think of all that might go wrong for her if she went out with him. "Lucy will also have to agree to being watched by someone she doesn't know."

"Of course. I understand." He flung his free arm around Harriet's shoulder and gave her a quick sideways squeeze. "If you tell her my sister makes excellent crepes, I'm sure she'll agree."

Harriet grinned. It was nice having a friend like Oliver, and it felt good being referred to as someone's best mate. For too long, she'd felt so abandoned and alone. Knowing Oliver, James, and Matthew could be relied on if she needed help was a blessing.

"I'm sure you're correct," Harriet said. "But I'll want to meet your sister first, if that's all right."

"Sure thing." Oliver withdrew his arm and sent her a broad smile. "Let me know when and I'll make it happen. Will give us a chance to discuss Mary Wilkes."

Harriet instinctively rolled her eyes and groaned in response to the mention of the girl Mr. Hudson employed as a cleaning lady "I'd rather not."

"You know she fancies you, right?"

"I do." She'd have to be blind and deaf to be unaware of the fact since Mary wasn't the least bit subtle.

"So why don't you make your move, Harry?"

"Make my move?" Harriet had no desire to venture down this conversational path.

Unfortunately, Oliver was quite determined. "I saw your expression when James mentioned the brothel and we were talking about our experiences of that nature. Made me realize you might not have much. Which is nothing to be embarrassed about, I assure you."

"To be honest," Harriet muttered, her face

turning hot with discomfort, "I've more important things to consider."

"Most people do, but that doesn't mean you can't make time for yourself on occasion. And Mary's extremely pretty. Shapely too. Don't you think?"

"Certainly, but I'm not in the business of taking a young woman's innocence."

Oliver snorted. "That girl is about as innocent as a seasoned courtesan. Mark my word, you'll not be her first or even her second. That's for sure."

Harriet struggled to keep the shock from her voice when she asked, "How on earth do you know that?"

"Saw her with David Bates last week in the back alley. Seemed to be having a jolly good time, if you know what I mean."

Baffled and slightly disgusted, Harriet shook her head. "In other words, she's giving herself to other men while pursuing me?"

"What can I say? Men aren't the only ones with needs of that nature."

Increasingly concerned about having to chat about this at greater length, Harriet regretted agreeing to speak with Lucy about going out with Oliver one evening. But at least her sister could serve as a reason for her to decline. Something could always come up, like a tummy ache or an unwillingness to sacrifice one precious evening with Harriet.

"I'll see you tomorrow," Harriet said when they

reached the next street corner where she would turn right while Oliver continued for two more blocks.

"Have a good evening." His arm came around her, drawing her into a tight embrace before letting her go. "Get some rest."

"You too," she said before stepping down from the pavement and crossing the street. The bakery up ahead would provide the pies she intended to purchase for supper.

"How was your day?" she asked Lucy when she returned to their lodgings.

"Boring as usual," Lucy complained. She sat at the table – the only other piece of furniture present besides two chairs and their beds – reading the book Harriet's friend Emily Brooke had provided during their last book club meeting.

Harriet had learned of the meetings from Ada Quinn, whose acquaintance she'd made in child-hood. They'd grown up near the same village, so they'd met every Sunday at church. As they'd grown up, their friendship had deepened. They'd kept in touch after Ada's father died and she'd moved to London. When Harriet herself had arrived a few years later, she'd sought her out.

At Ada's insistence, Harriet had joined her for one of the book club meetings, which took place the first Saturday morning of every month and was started by Emily, a viscount's daughter and the most upper-class person Harriet knew. Initially, Harriet's short hair had caused a bit of a stir in the group, but her explanation pertaining to practicality had apparently made enough sense for the issue to quickly be dropped.

The meetings took place during the only time Harriet had free from work and offered a lovely escape from the pretense she lived on a daily basis.

"Did you do the sums I prepared?" she asked Lucy.

"Yes, but I struggled with the last ones. The directions you left me were hard to follow."

"I'll go over it with you once we've eaten." Harriet collected the two single plates they owned and set them on the table. It helped that her sister was of an age now where she could at least help with basic house work. Like ensuring the space was swept once a day, the beds made, the surfaces cleaned, and the washing up done so Harriet didn't have to complete these chores when she returned home.

As was often the case, it was past ten o'clock before she was able to climb into bed, exhausted, and well aware that she'd only get four hours of sleep before she had to get up again and start a new day.

"Good night," she whispered before turning the light down.

"Good night," Lucy answered.

Harriet listened to her sister's gentle breathing until it slowed and then willed herself to fall asleep too. But doing so was a struggle. Her thoughts kept returning to her conversation with Oliver, to his mention of Mary, and to his opinion of Mr. Evans, which reminded her of her own encounter with the man yesterday.

It was silly of her to go over it all again, but she honestly couldn't help it. He'd made an impression. His touch had seared her. Just thinking of him made her heart beat faster. And while she'd done what she could to avoid him today, she couldn't deny that she harbored a secret desire for their paths to cross again soon. If only for her to experience once more the jolt of pleasure he'd caused.

But whatever hopes she might have allowed herself to have in this regard were disappointed during the next few days when work got in the way. Kept busy in the printing room, she had no cause to venture into the front of the building where Mr. Evans would likely be found.

This changed the following week when Harriet went to inform Mr. Hudson that they were beginning to run low on ink. Mr. Evans, whose desk was located near Mr. Hudson's greeted her politely when she arrived in the front office, the brief attention he gave her instantly flipping her stomach.

Despite her flustered state, she managed to keep her voice level while wishing him a good afternoon in return. She then turned to her employer, ever conscious of Mr. Evans and the searing effect he had on her nerves.

Fearful Mr. Hudson might catch her blushing, she fled back to the print room as soon as she'd relayed her message, but it took a good while before her pulse slowed to a normal pace. Wanting to see Mr. Evans again had clearly been foolish. She ought to forget him and focus on work.

A sound decision that fell apart the next day day when the door to the print room opened while she was assembling a sort. Harriet didn't look up from her work, but a prickly sensation at the nape of her neck alerted her to Mr. Evans's presence. It was the most bizarre experience yet.

"Mr. Michaels?" he asked, his firm voice sending a shiver across her shoulders. "A word, if I may?"

"Just a moment," Harriet informed him. "Give me the next word, Oliver."

Oliver did as she asked so she could finish the form she'd been working on. She slid it across to James who began adding ink while Matthew placed paper in the printing frame.

Harriet stood, rolled her shoulders, and stretched her back. "Mind if we take a five-minute break?"

Oliver glanced at Mr. Evans, then returned his attention to Harriet. He shrugged. "If you like."

Something in his tone suggested he wasn't pleased by the interruption. Harriet didn't blame him. They usually ran to the end of a chapter before taking a break, yet they'd only completed half.

She gave him an apologetic look. "I'll be right back."

"Sorry to interrupt," Mr. Evans said once they'd stepped out into the narrow transitional space between the print room and the front office. A door to the right led to the privy while another opened up to a modest storage room where Mary kept her cleaning supplies. "I've been meaning to speak with you for a couple of days but never found the chance to. Eventually I decided to seek you out."

It was ridiculous how much pleasure this remark gave her. She actually had to make a conscious effort to keep from grinning, since that would surely put Mr. Evans off.

So she crossed her arms and attempted a casual look. "Really?"

"The way we met keeps nagging at me," Mr. Evans explained. "I'd really like to make it up to you in some way by taking you out for a drink."

Harriet almost laughed. Her life had truly taken a turn toward satire when not only one but two attractive men were vying for her attention, while thinking she was a man. Honestly, she'd never before been so popular as she was as the working-class Mr. Harry Michaels, instead of the gently bred *Miss* Harriet Michaels.

Had she known, she might have taken to dressing like a man long ago.

"Thank you. That's very kind of you, but I really can't spare the time."

Mr. Evans met her gaze and held it for a moment before eventually nodding. "Fair enough. I just didn't want your only impression of me to be based on my constant knack for shoving you sideways."

She couldn't help but send him a cheeky smile while saying, "I'm afraid it's too late, Mr. Evans. The damage is already done."

His answering chuckle warmed her heart and made her feel strangely at ease with him. In a comforting sort of way that was wholly unexpected. "Hopefully, with time, that will change. After all, I do have my reputation to consider. If word of my awkwardness were to get out, I'd be socially ruined."

She laughed and the door from the print room opened.

"We ought to get back to work," Oliver said.

Harriet nodded. She bit her lip and gave Mr. Evans a hesitant look before saying, "Don't worry, your secret's safe with me."

"Thank you, Mr. Michaels. We'll leave it at that then, shall we?"

"Indeed." She followed Oliver back into the print room and went to prepare for the next set of sorts.

"What secret?" Oliver asked as he took his seat.

"Nothing." She waved one hand. "Don't worry about it."

"You're blushing, Harry." His voice was quiet but firm.

Harriet stilled. Her mind raced. She had to think of something to say to dismiss whatever suspicions Oliver might be having. Eventually, she shrugged. "I'm simply a bit overheated, that's all. Perhaps we should open another window?"

She deliberately tugged at her cravat for added effect and avoided glancing in Oliver's direction, fearful he'd see much more than he ought if he caught her gaze in that moment. Instead she busied herself with tidying up some of the forms she'd given to James earlier. He'd set them to the left of where she worked, so she didn't have to go get them herself.

Thankfully, Oliver did as she suggested without further comment. Their work resumed and Harriet relaxed.

"Did you speak with your sister?" Oliver asked at the end of the day.

"I did," Harriet slowly informed him. "She's not very keen on spending time with a stranger, but I'll do what I can to convince her."

"Let me know once you do. The Ugly Grouse has an excellent fiddler on Thursday evenings. It would be great if we could go listen to him together."

Harriet quite liked that idea, but once again, she worried it might overcomplicate matters. Still, she smiled and nodded as though in agreement. "I'd enjoy that."

"See you tomorrow," James said as he headed out.

"I'm off too," Matthew said.

"You coming?" Oliver asked once the others were gone.

"In a bit," Harriet said, hoping to avoid having to walk with him again. His eagerness for a closer relationship with her would only lead to trouble. Already, she feared, she'd revealed too much without thinking. The same was true of Mr. Evans. In future, she had to avoid both men to the best of her ability. "You go ahead."

Oliver hesitated, but when Harriet turned her back to him and proceeded to check the print they'd produced that afternoon, he wished her a pleasant evening and left.

She counted to ten after hearing the door swing shut, before sagging against the back of her chair. Pinching the bridge of her nose, she tossed the papers she'd been reviewing aside before raking her hair with her fingers. Good lord. The last thing she wanted to do was hurt Oliver's feelings, but better that than run the risk of him finding out she'd deceived everyone, including him.

Just to be sure he wouldn't be waiting for her outside, Harriet chose to stay in the print room a while longer. Which wasn't much of a chore since there was plenty to keep her busy.

She was in the process of tying the last of the bundled manuscripts together to save Richard the extra work tomorrow when the door leading out to the hallway opened and Mary appeared.

"Mr. Michaels. I'm glad to see you're still here. It must be a week since I saw you last."

Harriet suppressed a groan and tried to return Mary's smile while instinctively backing up a step. "Good to see you, Mary. You, er…look well."

Mary's cheeks pinkened and her expression appeared slightly bashful, though Harriet imagined it might be an act. Especially if what Oliver had said about her was true. "Ever the gentleman you are, Mr. Michaels. I must say, you're even more handsome than usual today, what with your hair all scruffy and such."

She set the broom she'd brought with her aside and swept toward Harriet with too much determination for Harriet's liking. Unfortunately, the work table directly behind her stopped her from retreating farther, allowing Mary to reach her within a few paces.

Harriet leaned back as Mary stepped forward, straight into her personal space.

"I wonder if you might be willing to add a bit of distance, Mary. You're awfully close."

Instead of retreating, Mary caught the lapels of Harriet's jacket and pulled her toward her. "I've been hoping to get you alone for a while now, Mr. Michaels. You're a difficult man to catch."

"Possibly because I don't wish to be caught," Harriet said while struggling to free herself from Mary's grasp.

"Let's put an end to the pretense, shall we? I mean, it's been fun and all, but you can only flirt with a girl for so long before you're expected to act."

What on earth was she on about? "I think you're mistaken, Mary. I've not been flirting."

"Sure you have." She chuckled and leaned in closer, her breath sweeping over the edge of Harriet's chin. "You're always smiling and praising my looks, thanking me for the work I do, and you even gave me a biscuit one time."

"I was being nice." Although in hindsight, Harriet could see she might have overdone it a notch. But she'd felt bad for Mary, having to clean up the mess made by nine men throughout the day. The privy was especially challenging. So she'd offered her a biscuit to make her feel better.

"You can dress it up however you like," Mary said, "but I know you're keen on my attentions. Once we've enjoyed each other's company, I'm sure you'll agree to a far more permanent attachment."

And before Harriet could manage the sidestep she'd hoped to achieve, Mary's mouth landed against her own. She sputtered and turned her head sideways. Ugh! Her first kiss, and it had to be with a girl.

"Come on, Mr. Michaels." The blasted creature was starting to undo her trousers.

"Stop it," Harriet choked. She'd been completely unprepared for such an assault. Her only thought in the moment was of escape. She grabbed Mary's wrists and shoved them aside. "Mary. I—"

The door to the print room opened again and Mr. Evans entered. "Sorry. I didn't realize…um…do carry on."

"Wait," Harriet called. "I was just coming to find you."

"You were?" Mr. Evans could not have sounded more surprised.

"You invited me for that drink, remember?" She managed to send him a pleading look over Mary's shoulder.

"Right. Of course."

"Sorry." Harriet met Mary's gaze full on. "I've got to go. If you don't mind."

"I rather do," Mary said, "but I suppose we can always resume our tryst later."

Harriet sent her gaze skyward. Heaven help her.

Perhaps a tougher approach was required. Clearly good manners were working against her in this particular instance. "Let's not."

"But—"

"My wife would not approve," Harriet said, latching onto the single most convincing argument she could think of for a man to avoid a pretty woman's attentions.

Mary blinked. "Oh. I'm terribly sorry. I didn't realize you were married."

"Rest assured, I'd gladly accept your…um…offer if I weren't." Harriet added a nod for good measure and managed to edge away from Mary. "I'll see you later. All right?"

She wished her a pleasant evening for good measure while grabbing her things and hurrying across to where Mr. Evans stood waiting. He also said goodbye to Mary before following Harriet through the building toward the front exit. They arrived on the street soon after, with neither saying a word until they'd walked several steps.

"I gather you're not keen on Mary then?" Mr. Evans finally asked, his cheerful tone prompting Harriet to laugh.

"Not in the least." She smirked. "You can have her, if you like."

"As generous as that is," he said, keeping his voice jovial, "I'd like to decline."

"The choice may not be up to you. Turns out, Mary can be very insistent." More so than Harriet had ever thought possible. She'd obviously underestimated her interest.

"Good thing I got there when I did."

Harriet heartily agreed. She shuddered at the thought of what might have happened if Mary had tried to grope her. "Thank you for showing up. And for agreeing to play along."

It was kind of him after she'd initially turned him down.

"You're welcome." Mr. Evans held her gaze for a second before jerking his head toward the left. "Come on. The place I have in mind is right over there."

CHAPTER SIX

Brody opened the door to the Ugly Grouse and led the way inside. The place was fairly crowded with working-class men intent on spending some time with their mates before going home to their families. Games of dice were being played at some tables. A small group had gathered for darts while others stood about chatting.

Brody surveyed the space. When he spotted a table for two in the far corner of the room, he suggested to Mr. Michaels they take it.

The young man, who'd been glancing around wide-eyed as though he'd never been in a place like this before, gave a quick nod. Stepping in front of him, Brody cleared a path to the table and gestured toward one of the chairs. He wasn't sure why he waited for Mr. Michaels to sit before claiming his own seat, and chose not to wonder about it further.

There were more important things to consider right now, like getting some drinks.

He raised his hand to catch the barmaid's attention. It took a while for her to arrive at their table, during which Brody asked Mr. Michaels if he'd also care for some food.

"No thank you," he replied. "I can't stay long."

"Got to get back to that wife you mentioned?" Brody asked, his voice deliberately teasing.

Mr. Michaels smiled and for a second, Brody could have sworn the entire tavern lit up with the brightness of ten thousand stars.

"I only said that so Mary would leave me alone."

Brody slowly nodded. He felt both stunned and muddled, as though someone had clubbed him over the head. A quick shake helped him banish the odd response he'd just had. And then the barmaid arrived, offering further distraction.

"Is pale ale all right with you?" Brody asked Mr. Michaels. When he gave a quick nod Brody ordered a couple of mugs.

"Anything else?" asked the barmaid, a buxom brunette with a saucy gleam in her eyes.

"No. That'll be all."

"Let me know if you change your mind, aye?" She added a wink before sauntering off with what looked like a very deliberate sway to her hips.

Brody glanced at Mr. Michaels, whose cheeks

had turned pink. "I'm starting to get the sense that forward women unnerve you."

"Not at all." Mr. Michaels crossed his arms and leaned back in his chair, appearing to affect a nonchalant pose without managing it very well. "It never ceases to surprise me when they behave in that way. After all, girls are brought up to protect their virtue."

"Some are, but not all. Unfortunately many are forced to supplement their income through the art of seduction. Or to make their entire living that way."

"It's a shame."

"I'm not sure they'd all agree with you there. Take Mary and that barmaid for instance. I believe they like the experience as much as the men they engage."

"Really?"

Mr. Michaels did not look convinced, which made Brody realize the young man was probably rather innocent with regards to the way of the world. A notion that instilled a sense of responsibility toward him.

Turning in his chair, he leaned forward and crossed his arms on the table. He met Mr. Michaels's gaze. Those eyes, a deep hazel, were so incredibly soulful. They could easily muddle men's minds if they belonged to a woman.

"Women can enjoy bed sport too," Brody said, in case the lad wasn't aware. "Take Mary for instance.

She wouldn't be begging for you to tup her if she didn't expect to find pleasure as well."

"I…um…"

The blush was back. Brighter than before despite the dim light in their corner. It was adorable, Brody mused, only to tamp down that inappropriate thought as soon as it formed.

He frowned. Perhaps if he spoke about bedding women he'd stop responding to Mr. Michaels in ways that were getting increasingly worrisome. "Most men gain their experience from loose women like her."

"They're not worried they'll get the pox?" Mr. Michaels whispered, so low Brody barely heard him.

The barmaid returned with their order, setting two tankards on the table. Brody picked his up as soon as she was gone and waited for Mr. Michaels to do the same. "To new acquaintances."

Mr. Michaels echoed his words and took a sip, his eyes widening with surprise as the ale slid down his throat.

"You've never had ale before?" Brody asked, once again puzzled by the younger man's inexperience with things he himself had been introduced to by the age of fifteen.

"Of course I have," Mr. Michaels said, his voice breaking enough to reveal a higher pitched sound for a second. He cleared his throat, and when he spoke again, he did so in the lower tone Brody had grown accustomed to. "I'm used to a different flavor, that's all. I actually prefer this. It's really good."

"Glad to hear it." Satisfaction settled somewhere deep within Brody's chest. It felt like his heart was expanding with warmth and... Best return to the previous subject of conversation. "About your concern, any man with an ounce of brain will make sure to use a French letter."

"I see."

Noting Mr. Michaels' puzzled expression, Brody had to ask, "You do know what a French letter is?"

"Of course."

Brody frowned. It didn't sound like the lad had a clue, which could prove dangerous for him if he decided to seek out the wrong sort of woman.

"It's a sheath made from pig skin." When Mr. Michaels stared at him as though with incomprehension, Brody decided to add, "Men can put them on their rods to protect themselves and the women they bed, both from unwanted pregnancy and from disease. Apothecaries carry them."

Clearly, this was news to Mr. Michaels. The poor lad looked like he might be in need of smelling salts soon. Which was also rather odd. It was common behavior for men to engage in casual discourse with each other. He did so himself all the time. At Eton and Oxford, the lads had not held back with regard to crass language or subjects relating to sexual experience. Not once had any of them appeared shocked.

If anything, it had been considered normal male behavior, as long as it never took place in the presence of women. So it was strange to meet a young man of roughly eighteen or nineteen years of age who balked at such things. The only explanation was he didn't have close male friends and wasn't accustomed to such conversations.

Taking pity, Brody said, "I'm sorry if speaking of such things offends you. My only intention was to make sure you're well informed."

"Ah… Thank you. I'm…er…much obliged."

Mr. Michaels reached for his ale and drank a fare measure while Brody tried to think of something else to discuss. Something more appropriate perhaps? "I'm curious. How did you become a compositor at Hudson & Co.?"

Relief softened Mr. Michaels's expression. He was clearly glad to have moved away from the previous subject. "I came to London a couple of years ago. After Papa died."

"I'm sorry," Brody murmured with genuine sympathy. "The death of a parent is hard. My own father died when I was roughly your age."

"My regrets," Mr. Michaels said. His hand moved toward Brody's, only to halt mid motion. Snatching it back, he said, "My sister and I lost everything when it happened. The only solution was to find work, but our village had little to offer in that regard. So I decided to come to London where I believed there'd be more opportunities."

"You didn't inherit anything?"

"No." Rather than elaborate, Mr. Michaels quickly said, "I've always been fond of books. They fascinate me. All the knowledge and information packed between those pages. The stories that can take you to faraway places or let you experience things you'd not be able to otherwise. Books are a gift to the world, Mr. Evans, and I wanted to have a part in creating them."

The wonder with which he spoke was spellbinding. "You've certainly achieved that."

Mr. Michaels nodded. "I started out at Hudson & Co. as a delivery boy. When George, the previous compositor, left on account of better pay elsewhere, Mr. Hudson gave James, Matthew, and Oliver a chance to try out for the position before placing an advertisement in the paper. I asked if I could try as well, and instead of snubbing me, Mr. Hudson gave me the opportunity I needed to prove myself."

"He strikes me as a really good man," Brody said.

"He is. Gave me the job on the spot and hired a new boy to do the deliveries."

"And your colleagues don't mind that you got the job instead of them?"

Mr. Michael's shrugged. "No. James and Matthew can't sit still. They need to move, so working the press is perfect for them. As for Oliver, he's happy avoiding the responsibility placed on my shoulders. And besides, none of their fingers are slim enough to place the sorts with the sort of precision I'm capable of."

"Sounds reasonable," Brody said, his gaze instinctively going to Mr. Michaels's hand, which did appear rather petite. Another curiosity, considering his age. It was as though parts of him belonged to a young adolescent, not someone who'd reached the cusp of manhood. Could it be that he'd lied about his age?

That would explain why Mary's advance might have scared him.

"How about you?" Mr. Michaels inquired.

Brody stared at him for a second. "What?"

"Why did you choose to become Mr. Hudson's assistant editor?" Mr. Michaels studied him with blatant curiosity. "When I happened upon you that first time, you didn't strike me as the sort of man who needs to work for a living. And if you do, I expect you'd need a higher salary than what Hudson & Co. can provide."

"Um…" Brody grabbed his tankard with both hands and considered coming up with some sort of excuse, only to decide the truth – or part of it, at least – might be better. "Looks can be deceiving, Mr. Michaels. Unfortunately, I'm not as well off as you might think. My fault, to some extent. A lapse in judgment I'm now trying to rectify."

Auspiciously, he had received an offer on the townhouse that morning, which he'd since accepted. The down payment alone would allow him to pay off the five hundred pounds Finn owed Mr. Apcot.

"Do you know," Mr. Michaels said with a mischievous smile. "You just got a lot more interesting. I'm intrigued."

A sentiment Brody shared, though he chose not to say as much. But the truth was he got a feeling things weren't quite as they seemed with Mr. Michaels either, and wondered what secrets the lad might be keeping.

"Another drink?" he asked once they'd both downed the last of their ale.

"Thank you, but I really must get home to my sister." Mr. Michaels stood, so Brody did too. "I'm glad we did this though. It was…nice."

Brody felt an indefinable pang of emotion behind his ribcage. It was the most curious sensation – a little too much like a yearning. It puzzled him as much as the fact that he'd taken note of the lad's lovely eyes, his elegant fingers, and luscious lips…

Good God. Brody froze as panic swept through him. He could not be attracted to Mr. Michaels. It was impossible. He fancied women. He'd *always* fancied women. Their sensual curves were what aroused him. Not bristly jawlines and muscular chests.

Although one might argue that Mr. Michaels was

quite clean shaven and didn't look muscular in the least, he'd still have all the wrong bits.

"Yes," Brody agreed, fearing he might sound strangled if he said more than one word at the moment. He added a smile for good measure while feeling a light sweat break out at the nape of his neck.

"I'll see you tomorrow then," Mr. Michaels said as soon as they were outside on the pavement. "I'm headed in that direction. How about you?"

"The opposite," Brody informed him while doing his best to dismiss Mr. Michaels's pretty features. It was as though they were growing more apparent with each passing second. Perhaps because of the ale?

By the time he climbed into bed one hour later, he'd decided it had to be the drink. It was the only thing that made any sense.

CHAPTER SEVEN

An uneasy feeling settled over Harriet the next day as she worked. Oliver was unusually quiet. More than that, he responded to Harriet's comments with an underlying hint of contempt.

When she'd greeted him, he'd muttered a clipped, "Morning," without making eye contact with her. As he read from the manuscript, his voice was curt to the point where even James and Matthew exchanged wary glances.

It got worse as the day wore on. By the time work ended, Harriet could no longer stand the tense atmosphere filling the print room.

Determined to get to the bottom of it, she grabbed Oliver's arm and held him back, preventing him from following James and Matthew when they left. "What's wrong?"

Oliver shrugged. "Nothing."

"Really?" Harriet scoffed. "If I've said or done something to upset you, I'd rather you confront me about it instead of treating me with hostility. So what's got you in a snit, Oliver?"

With his jaw set in a hard line, Oliver looked as though stubbornness might win out. Harriet sighed and withdrew her hand. She shook her head and began turning away when Oliver seized her and spun her around. Her back connected with the closed door, and Oliver leaned in, his eyes sparking with heightened emotion.

Harriet sucked in a breath. Her pulse, so steady moments before, now leapt with agitation.

"I saw you." Oliver's voice shook. His nostrils flared as he gritted his teeth. "You said you had to get home to your sister, but that was clearly a lie. Wasn't it?"

Harriet frowned. "I don't follow."

Oliver snorted. A pained expression captured his features. "I saw you last night. With Mr. Evans."

"You left here at least ten minutes before me, so unless…" A sick sensation swirled in Harriet's stomach. "Were you stalking me?"

"Don't be absurd. I realized I'd forgotten my hat, so I returned. Right in time to find you heading into The Ugly Grouse with Mr. Evans." Oliver held Harriet's gaze. "Apparently you had no issue enjoying a drink with him. Me, on the other hand, the idiot you've been leading on for the past couple of months, gets the boot."

Panic descended on Harriet with the weight of an anvil. He had to know she wasn't male. Somehow, in her eagerness to befriend him, she must have overplayed her hand. It was the only possible explanation. And yet, instinct compelled her to keep up her ruse - to try and convince him he'd made a mistake.

So she did what she could to convey incredulity. "Leading you on? I'm a lad, Oliver, in case you weren't aware."

"Aye. I'm aware all right." Oliver's fingertips grazed her jaw as he pressed up against her. "Don't pick him, Harry. Pick me."

Confusion plunged Harriet's brain into a fog-like state as Oliver's mouth met hers. He was kissing her, even though he thought she was male, which was not only strange, but also highly illegal. Were it not for the fact that she was indeed a woman.

She'd barely managed to process this before something distracted her from it. Not the kiss, which she meant to put an end to with a hard shove, but something wet and sticky in her snuggly fitted trousers.

Oh no. Not now.

She placed her palm on Oliver's chest and pushed him until he was forced to retreat.

A pained expression filled his eyes. "Not good enough for you?"

"It's got nothing to do with that."

"He's too fancy, you know. That sort of man will set his sights higher than on a compositor with ink-stained fingers. Provided he even leans that way."

Although the comment was made in anger, Harriet knew it was true. As much as it stung, she had more important things to consider right now. "I need to use the privy."

Oliver gave her an odd look. "Right now?"

"Yes." She shoved her way past him and ran to her bag, acutely aware that her situation was not getting any better.

"What the hell, Harry?" He fell quiet for a moment as she tore her bag open and started rummaging through her things, searching for the cotton padding she always carried with her. And then… "It looks like your trousers are stained. Did you sit in something?"

"No." She was always so careful to pay attention to when she might next expect her courses, but she'd been busy and distracted lately, and if she wasn't mistaken, they'd come a bit early.

"Well, it looks like you've pissed yourself," Oliver stated with a chuckle.

Harriet muttered an oath. "I haven't…"

She gritted her teeth as she realized her bag did not contain the supplies she needed. Brilliant! Closing her eyes, she tried to figure out what to do next. She could perhaps use a cravat in a pinch, though she'd need more than one if she were to hold everything in place.

Swallowing, she settled on the best course of action and glanced at Oliver. Now that she knew his secret, she was certain he'd keep hers as well. It might even make him feel better if he were to find out she didn't appeal as much as he'd thought. Unless he felt betrayed on account of her deception.

Never mind that. Time was of the essence. She couldn't afford to question herself any longer.

"I need your help," she said, hoping he'd make this easy on her.

He snorted. "First you reject me and then you come running. A fine friend you are, Harry."

"My name isn't Harry."

He gave her a puzzled look before rolling his eyes and shaking his head. "Sure it is."

"No. It isn't. It's Harriet." When all he did was give her a blank stare, she admitted. "I'm not male like you think. I'm female, and I've just gotten my courses. That's why my trousers are stained."

His eyes widened as his face turned ashen. "You're not joking?"

"I'm not. Please, Oliver, I need your cravat." She sighed when all he did was stare at her in mute silence. "I'll be sure to buy you a new one. Promise."

"All right." Moving stiffly, he undid the knot, unwound the length of linen from around his neck, and handed it to her, his hand trembling.

"Thank you." She grabbed the cravat and ran for the privy. "Be right back."

When she returned some five minutes later, Oliver was sitting on a stool, hugging himself while he stared at the floor. Hearing her enter the room, he glanced in her direction, blinked rapidly, and rushed to his feet. Pausing as though unsure of what to do next, he studied her with alarm.

"Are you sure you're not male?" he eventually asked.

She produced a startled laugh. "Positive."

He didn't appear to share her humor. "You look like a young man."

Frowning, she tilted her head. "I'm not sure if I should be glad about that or offended."

His expression turned increasingly wary and when he spoke next, his voice sounded shaky. "How bad would it be for you if I were to mention your secret to Mr. Hudson?"

"He'd probably sack me, leaving me without an income. My only reason for pretending was so I could get this job. The work available to women is either demeaning or doesn't pay well. With a younger sister to care for, I have to earn more than what I would as a shop assistant or maid. Working here made that possible, especially once I proved my worth."

"So it's fair to say you'd like to prevent me from

letting it slip that you're not Mr. Harry Michaels but rather Miss Harriet Michaels?"

"Very much so."

Leaning against the stool on which he'd been sitting, he drew a ragged breath. The fear he experienced at knowing he hadn't revealed himself to a likeminded man but to someone who might choose to use his proclivity against him was understandable. The danger he faced if anyone learned the truth about him could not be disputed.

Sympathizing, Harriet placed her hand on his arm and gently assured him, "Your secret is safe with me, Oliver. I promise not to betray you."

He pressed his lips together and nodded while staring at her with glistening eyes. "Thank you. I'll keep your confidence too."

She nodded her appreciation then grabbed her bag along with her cap. "If it's all right with you, I've got to get going. This make-shift compress I've fashioned will only last so long."

He made a face and appeared to shake off the panic he'd been subjected to. "Can we please speak of something else?"

She grinned as she preceded him through the door. "Name the subject."

"How about your tendre for Mr. Evans?"

Harriet shot him a disgruntled look. "I can't imagine what you're talking about."

"Can't you?" Oliver asked. He quietly added,

"There's a reason seeing you with him last night made me jealous."

Her hand grabbed his arm, drawing him to a halt so she could face him. "I'm sorry, Oliver. Had I truly been male with…that sort of inclination, I'm sure I would have welcomed your interest."

A faint smile tugged at his lips. "Thank you. I've got to say, I still can't believe you managed to fool me. Now that I've had some time to come to terms with the truth and take a better look at you, it's obvious to me you're a woman. Your features are simply too delicate."

"People tend to see what they expect. I counted on that when I showed up dressed in men's clothes with my hair cropped short and said my name was Harry." They resumed walking. "I was terribly nervous – wasn't sure I'd manage to pull it off – but I knew I had to hide my concerns and appear confident if I was going to manage."

"No one suspected a thing, which is very impressive."

"You don't feel betrayed?"

He seemed to reflect on that question a moment. "No. You did what you had to do and for good reason. Who am I to be angry about that? I mean, I'll not deny being disappointed since I fancied Harry, but you and I are friends first and foremost. I hope that won't change even if you're a woman."

"Of course not. I'll always value your friendship."

"And as your friend, I'd love to know how you intend on pursuing Mr. Evans."

Harriet nearly choked on her own tongue. "I've no intention of—"

"Come off it, Harry – and yes, I intend to keep using that name since it suits you – Mr. Evans is handsome and charming."

"You said he'd never look twice at someone of my station."

"Aha! So you do have an interest." When Harriet rolled her eyes he confessed, "That comment was made when I hoped to convince you to give him up in favor of me. I no longer have such a wish."

She sighed. "It matters not if I find him handsome or charming. He thinks I'm a man and that won't change."

"Are you certain?"

"Quite." It was bad enough that Oliver knew the truth about her. Trusting additional people with it would just increase the risk of everyone else finding out. It wasn't a chance she would take for any reason – certainly not for a chance at something as hard to come by as love.

CHAPTER EIGHT

I t was starting to dawn on Brody that getting paid to read might be the best job in the world. He was able to sit back, relax, and dive into a story that hadn't yet been released to the world. It was much like being an explorer, embarking on some new adventure without knowing what to expect.

For the most part, the submissions he worked his way through weren't very enticing. Finding those he imagined the masses would find appealing took time. But this did give him hope for the book he and his friends had written, for it was surely better than most of what was in his slush pile.

A week had now passed since he'd started at Hudson & Co., and he decided the time had come for him to address his reason for being there in the first place. So when he arrived at work, he took a moment to greet everyone and prepare a pot of tea for himself. Once this was done, he settled into his chair and, using his desk as a shield, retrieved the manuscript from his satchel.

He slipped it onto the top of the pile and started to read the familiar words. A grin pulled at his lips as Anthony's writing made him laugh. What a great visual this was, of the hero cursing his mother's meddlesome ways. The internal thoughts were hilarious, both acerbic and sarcastic.

Leaning back, he stretched out his legs, then crossed them at the ankles and turned the page. There was no doubt in his mind this writing was better than most of what he'd enjoyed this past week. Only two other manuscripts had shown promise, with neither being romantic in nature. He'd recommended both – a travel journal and an adventure novel - to Mr. Hudson.

One hour later, he'd finished perusing the first three chapters of *A Seductive Scandal*. Time to implement the next part of his plan. He straightened and set the manuscript on his desk. "This is really good."

"What is?" Mr. Hudson asked, his attention on a letter he appeared to be writing.

"This book." Brody stood, picked up the manuscript, and strode across to Mr. Hudson's desk. "It's a romance novel from what I gather, written with a touch of humor.

Mr. Hudson stilled. He set his quill aside and gave Brody his full attention. "Let me see."

Heart thumping harder than ever, Brody handed him the book he and his friends had pinned their dreams on. He held his breath as Mr. Hudson located the first page and started to read.

"Hmm…" He continued onto page two. "Yes. This does hold promise. With Miss Austen's death last year, the publishing industry has been clamoring for a new author of her capabilities. I'll take this home with me tonight and see if the rest is as good as the start. Thank you, Mr. Evans. This could prove a game changing find for us all."

A game changing find?

Brody bubbled with excitement. It was all he could do not to thank Mr. Hudson profusely. But that would probably look suspicious. So he did his best to maintain a calm demeanor. Adding a nod of acknowledgement, he moved away from Mr. Hudson's desk.

"Oh, one more thing," Mr. Hudson said, halting Brody's retreat. "I'd like to review the first test run of *Through the Jungle*. Mr. Michaels promised it would be ready today. Can you please fetch it for me?"

"Certainly." Brody exited the front office space and approached the print room.

He pushed the door open and paused in the doorway. On the previous occasions he'd come here, the room had either been quiet, the workers mostly gone for the day, or he'd been too intent on his purpose to notice the work taking place. He did so now, noting the two large men who worked the press. One was adding ink while another raised and lowered parts with the use of a lever. Paper was swept in and out of the contraption with expert speed and blocks of text imprinted on the fresh sheets.

To the right sat Mr. Michaels, together with another slightly older man who perched on a stool with a manuscript in his hands. It was the same chap who'd come to fetch Mr. Michaels when Brody had tried to invite him out for a drink. The chap read while Mr. Michaels prepared the blocks of text to be printed.

Brody stared. The grace of the young man's movements, the swiftness with which he completed the task and had the block sent to the press, was a marvel to behold.

Unwilling to interrupt, he kept quiet until a natural break emerged when the man who was reading moved to the next page.

Brody cleared his throat. "Forgive the intrusion, but Mr. Hudson asked me to fetch the first copy of *Through the Jungle*. He believes it ought to be ready?"

Mr. Michaels's gaze met his and held for a couple of seconds, as though it took time for his brain to acknowledge Brody's presence. He suddenly blinked. "Right. Of course. I'll, um…"

"If you point me in the right direction I can fetch it," Brody said.

"I'm actually feeling like it might be time for a break," the man who'd been reading announced. He stood and stuck out his hand for Brody to shake. "We've not been properly introduced yet. I'm Oliver Tomkins, and those two blokes over there are James Dorsey and Matthew Jenkins."

Brody accepted the handshake. "Pleased to meet you."

"What say you?" Mr. Tomkins asked Mr. Michaels. "Shall we take ten minutes?"

Mr. Michaels frowned at his colleague. "Five is all we have time for with luncheon approaching within the next hour."

"Good enough." The colleague headed toward the exterior door, calling for the other two men who wielded the press to join him. Within a few seconds, only Brody and Mr. Michaels remained.

"It's right over here," Mr. Michaels said, his gaze darting away from Brody as he started forward. In his rush, he must have forgotten to watch his step, for he didn't quite clear the stool on which his colleague had been sitting and promptly tripped.

Instinctively, Brody reached out and grabbed his arm, which forced him to notice two things. First, Mr. Michaels was slimly built beneath his wool jacket and shirt. Second, he lacked the muscle one might expect from a youth his age.

The lad stumbled to a sharp halt. Seeking to steady himself, he latched onto Brody's shoulder. He immediately snatched his hand away, though not before Brody was able to wonder at the way it felt. The fact that he found himself liking the added contact was rather disturbing.

"Sorry. That was incredibly clumsy of me."

"No need to apologize," Brody said while staring into Mr. Michaels's beautiful eyes. He gritted his teeth. Surely this wasn't normal, for a man to pay attention to another man's eyes.

Thankfully Mr. Michaels averted his gaze in the next instant and pushed his way past Brody. "It's right here."

"What is?"

"The book."

"Oh right. Of course." *Idiot.* Brody cleared his throat. "I couldn't help but notice the skill with which you were working before. I've never seen anything like it."

Mr. Michaels turned and directed a radiant smile at him. It was enough to knock any mortal off his feet. "Just goes to show that one can do anything with enough determination."

"You're referring to your background and the lack of expectation it might have led to?"

"Precisely."

This was said so quickly Brody wondered if this was indeed what Mr. Michaels had meant. Instead of remarking on it, he decided to add to their conversation by saying, "I must admit I share your belief.

While life is certainly easier for the wealthy, there are opportunities for those who aren't. Provided one is creative enough."

Mr. Michaels gave him an odd look. "You don't…"

"What?"

"It's nothing." Mr. Michaels held the book toward Brody. "Once Mr. Hudson gives this his stamp of approval, we'll schedule the number of copies he wants us to make."

Brody wanted to know what Mr. Michaels had left unsaid, but he sensed the lad would rather he didn't, so he left the subject alone. Taking the book, he tried to ignore the jolt he experienced when Mr. Michaels's fingers touched his.

His pulse leapt with the sort of excitement that made him very afraid.

"Thank you," he managed and took a step back, adding a safe amount of distance. He'd thought to ask Mr. Michaels if he might like to meet for another drink after work, but decided it might be best not to.

The way Mr. Michaels watched him, his lips slightly parted in wonder, was further cause for concern. Spending additional time together would be unwise. Whatever was happening here, it had to end. At once.

Disturbed by his increased responsiveness toward the young man, he backed toward the door, wished him a pleasant rest of the day, and fled to the safety of his desk.

"Begging your pardon, sir," Rhys told Brody that evening while he enjoyed an after-dinner drink in his study. "The Marquess of Ramsgate wishes to see you."

Brody stared at his butler. "The marquess is here?"

"Indeed. Shall I show him in or would you rather I tell him you're not at home?"

"By all means, show him in." The butler departed and Brody stood in anticipation of Ramsgate's arrival. He couldn't imagine what might have brought the man to his home at such a late hour. They weren't exactly friends, the marquess being a good twenty years Brody's senior.

"I hope you can forgive me for interrupting your evening," Ramsgate said when he entered the room, "but I fear it could not be helped."

"It's quite all right," Brody said. "I've completed my dinner and have no further plans besides enjoying a glass of brandy before I retire. Would you care for some?"

Ramsgate gave a curt nod. "Please."

Brody prepared the drink and handed it over, then gestured toward the armchair adjacent to the one he himself had occupied earlier. "Won't you sit?"

A brief hesitation suggested Ramsgate's reluctance to get too comfortable, which in turn put Brody on edge. He forced a smile and settled into his own chair as soon as the other man was seated, and angled himself toward him. "I believe this is the first time you've come here since I became duke."

"Yes." Ramsgate took a quick sip of his brandy while knitting his brow. Discomfort was etched in every aspect of his expression. "A courtesy, you understand, in deference to your rank within Society."

This remark did little to quash Brody's rising concerns. Nevertheless, he did his best to feign calmness, even though it felt like his nerves were so tightly drawn they might snap. "Do enlighten me."

Ramsgate took yet another sip then set his drink aside on the table between the two chairs. "The matter at hand pertains to your brother."

Oh dear. What now?

"He attended a dinner at Vauxhall Gardens last night," Ramsgate continued. "I was there too, with my daughters and… Well, the fact of the matter is, he and my youngest, Fiona, were separated from our small group while watching the waterfall spectacle. I can't really blame them. There were a great many people present. Trouble is, rather than wait with

Fiona to one side until it was over, your brother swept her away between the trees."

Brody went very still. A sick sensation crawled through him. It took some effort to force the next words out. "Are you saying he made advances upon her?"

Of course that was what he was saying.

"They were seen, you understand, so although it was merely a kiss - and I say merely because I'm aware it could have been worse - I had little choice. I had to respond."

"Of course. If you're worried my brother won't do his duty, you may rest assured that he shall. I'll see to the special license myself if you wish."

"You misunderstand," Ramsgate muttered. He glanced at his glass of brandy but refrained from reaching for it. When his gaze returned to Brody's, there was a very distinct degree of regret in his eyes. "I've always held your family in the highest regard. Your father was a good friend, whose loss still pains me. That said, your brother is not the sort of man I wish to have as a son-in-law."

Of course not. No one wanted their daughter to marry a man who enjoyed high stakes gambling and lost every time, or the sort who drank to excess and was often seen with some sort of harlot upon his arm.

"But if you're not looking for him to save your daughter's reputation through marriage, what then?"

"I'm here to inform you that I have issued a challenge in Fiona's honor. She has no brothers, so the duty falls upon me. All things considered, I thought it best to let you know, to be sure your brother shows up once the time and location for the duel have been determined."

Brody stared at the marquess while doing his best not to gape. How could Finn have neglected to mention this to him? Granted, they'd not crossed paths since yesterday afternoon, but he could have left a note. Something to the effect of:

Oh by the way, Brother, I decided to defile Lord Ramsgate's daughter, so there's a good chance he'll put me in the ground the next time we meet.

Brody blinked.

Unsure of how to respond in the moment, he stalled for time by setting his glass to his lips and allowing the brandy to slide down his throat. The warm sensation that followed was welcome, but didn't do much to ease his concerns.

"Must you resort to such drastic measures?" He knew the words were wrong the moment he spoke them. Still, he had to try and dissuade the man from the course of action he'd chosen.

Ramsgate looked appropriately appalled. "We're speaking of my daughter's ruination at the hands of a man whose character leaves a great deal to be desired."

It was Brody's turn to take issue. "Finn may have

his flaws, I'll admit, but I won't permit you to speak ill of him while in my home."

"Very well." Ramsgate sat for a moment in silence, then grabbed his glass and downed the remainder of his drink. He stood and proceeded to pace, his expression darkening by the second. "I would have believed myself too old for this, but I cannot allow the matter to slide. Justice must be sought if reputations are to be upheld. Surely you understand this?"

"I do. I simply wish there might be another way."

"There isn't. Not one I can think of. Especially not when the first strains of gossip are already making their rounds. I must act swiftly – Losturn must be put in his place."

"I can speak with him," Brody tried, "convince him to make a public apology."

"Are you jesting, Your Grace?" When Brody flattened his lips and shook his head in shame, Ramsgate came to a halt before him and said, "You've no idea what this is like since you have no children, but try to imagine how you might feel if you were in my shoes."

The answer came to Brody before he could blink. He'd kill the bastard.

As if reading his mind, Ramsgate told him stiffly, "You may rest assured, I've no desire to take your brother from you, Corwin. First blood will do."

The words eased Brody's mind a great deal. "I'll

inform my brother of your visit and what you have said."

Ramsgate gave a curt nod. "I'll send a note as soon as I've decided on a time and place."

"Of course." Sensing an end to the interview, Brody stood. "I'll be his second."

"Thank you, Your Grace."

Brody summoned his butler as soon as Ramsgate was gone. "Did my brother say where he was going tonight?"

"I'm afraid not."

No chance of trying to find him and drag him home by his ear. "Please tell him to come and see me as soon as he returns. There's a matter he and I need to discuss."

Brody glanced at the clock. It was already nine. Given the fact that he was meant to start work at eight, he'd hoped to be on his way upstairs by now. Annoyed with Finn for causing such senseless trouble, he crossed to the sideboard instead and re-filled his glass.

It was almost one by the time he heard the front door. Having found a book with which to pass the time, Brody set it aside and waited for Finn to appear. He did so soon enough and was wearing the sort of wide grin that suggested he'd had a spectacular evening.

"Didn't expect to see you up at this hour," Finn said. He sauntered into the room and collapsed in the chair Ramsgate had used earlier. "But I'm glad you are since I no longer have to wait for tomorrow to tell you I've fallen in love."

Brody gnashed his teeth. "I only stayed up because there's an urgent matter we need to discuss."

"Miss Vaughn is the loveliest lady you'll ever meet."

"The Marquess of Ramsgate came to call a few hours ago," Brody said, his voice stiff as he leaned forward in his seat and pierced his brother with a hard glare. "I hear he's challenged you to a duel, Finn. Because you couldn't refrain from kissing his daughter in public."

"Well I—"

"How could you neglect to tell me this?"

Finn scratched his head and looked slightly sheepish. "Um…."

His blasé attitude only infuriated Brody more. "What the hell were you thinking?"

"I must confess I wasn't," Finn said, scratching his head in a sort of bemused way that only made Brody angrier. "She looked so pretty in the moonlight. I simply couldn't resist."

Brody stared at him. "You couldn't resist?"

"Afraid not."

"She's a marquess's daughter," Brody shouted, "not some trollop with whom you can have your way without consequence."

"Sorry, Brody. I realize this may have upset your evening but—"

"Upset my evening?" Brody shot to his feet, bringing his brandy glass with him and downing the contents in one fell swoop. His blood was boiling, heating his head until he felt a violent pain taking root at the base of his skull. "You've ruined a young lady's reputation."

"I did apologize to her father at the time. Considering his response, I rather thought he'd retracted the challenge and that the entire debacle had been forgotten."

Brody blinked. How was it possible for one person to be so bloody naïve? His own brother, no less? He returned his glass to the sideboard and shoved his hands into his pockets. "Although I did try to find another solution, marriage is out of the question. Ramsgate doesn't believe one kiss is sufficient grounds for you to ruin his daughter's life further."

"Meaning?"

"He doesn't consider you worthy of being her husband. Hence, the duel, since this is his only remaining course of action if he's to defend her honor and put you in your place."

This remark finally seemed to strike a chord with Finn. He straightened in his chair and positioned himself with his forearms resting upon his thighs, his attention fixed on the floor. "I've never been a very good shot or fencer."

"Thankfully, it's only to first blood. However, that doesn't rule out a stroke of bad luck. You can still be killed, which is why I intend to get you out of the country."

Finn's gaze snapped to his. The somber expression he wore now suggested some common sense did exist behind his usual carefree demeanor. "Absolutely not."

"You can go to America. Start a new life for yourself."

"I don't know anyone in America," Finn complained.

"You'll make friends in time, but at least you'll be alive."

"I'm sorry, Brody." Finn stood and planted his feet apart while crossing his arms. "Leaving is out of the question. This is my home – always has been. I'll die here if need be."

"Don't be an idiot."

Finn scowled. "I'm not. For once, I'm trying to do the right thing."

Brody scrubbed a hand over his face. "Why the hell couldn't you have decided to do so *before* kissing Lady Fiona?"

Or gambling away my money?

"Doing so would have been wisest, I'll agree. But

what's done is done and it's time for me to face the consequences of my actions."

"On a dueling field." Brody shook his head. "I trust you'll choose swords?"

Finn's answering nod was a small relief. "My marksmanship is abysmal, so that would be the prudent decision."

"I still intend to find a way out of this mess. For now, let's agree that your late-night diversions are over and done with." When Finn appeared on the verge of protesting, Brody informed him, "I cannot afford additional mishaps right now."

It took a moment for Finn to respond, but he finally nodded. "I understand."

"Good." Brody crossed to the door. "There's a plate of food for you in the dining room in case you're hungry. I myself am for bed since I've got to rise in five hours. I'll see you tomorrow after work. I expect you to be home then."

"I will be," Finn assured him. "Thank you, Brody."

Brody muttered a quick, "Goodnight," and left, no less worried about his brother's fate than he'd been a half hour earlier.

CHAPTER NINE

When Harriet woke, she went about her usual morning routine. Once dressed, she was about to set the table for breakfast when a low groan brought her attention to Lucy. She glanced at her sister just in time to watch her roll to her stomach and vomit onto the floor.

Harriet grabbed a bucket and rushed to her bedside. With gentle movements, she held her hair out of her sister's face while the poor girl continued to empty her stomach. When Lucy finally sighed and slumped against her bed, Harriet placed one hand on her brow. It was burning hot.

"Did you feel sick last night before bed or at any time during the night?" Harriet asked.

"No. Only now. My head hurts, and my stomach. I..." A distressed look filled her eyes and she suddenly leaned back over the side of the bed and vomited once more.

Not knowing why Lucy was sick since they'd had the same dinner, Harriet worried it might be something more serious than an upset stomach. She collected a glass of water and helped Lucy drink a little. She then cleaned up the mess on the floor while deciding what to do next. Ordinarily, she had to provide Mr. Hudson with advance notice if she required a day off work.

Lucy retched again and whimpered softly afterward in a clear show of pain.

Harriet checked her forehead once more, just to be sure. There was no mistaking the fever or the fact that Lucy was ill. These things happened. It wasn't anyone's fault, however inconvenient it was for a number of reasons. One being the cost of the doctor.

She opened the wardrobe and kneeled so she could retrieve the box she kept tucked away on the floor all the way at the back. It contained her savings – the money she had been putting toward the finishing school she hoped Lucy might one day attend. This was the plan – to provide Lucy the life that should have been hers, had their parents lived. It would now be delayed once more, but that couldn't be helped. Ensuring Lucy's health had to come first.

"I'm going to fetch the doctor. Would you like a piece of bread or a cup of tea before I go?"

Lucy shook her head. "Please hurry back."

"I will. I promise." She put on her cap and left, clattering down the stairs and bursting out onto the street in her haste to get help.

With two pounds tucked in her pocket, she hurried toward the end of the street and turned right. The doctor she'd used when Lucy had measles last year wasn't far. And he'd been fairly decent, Harriet thought. The advice he'd offered seemed to have helped at the time.

She turned a corner and crossed the street. The alleyway up ahead provided a shortcut. She darted along it, not noticing right away that a couple of scruffy men loitered at the far end, until one of them laughed.

Harriet came to a halt and considered her options. The men did not look the least bit good-natured, and now they were staring in her direction with a bit too much interest for her liking.

"Oi!" one of them called as he pushed away from the building he'd been leaning against. "Can we help you with something?"

Harriet shook her head, only slightly appeased by the fact that they'd think her a young man. "No thanks. I…um…think I took a wrong turn."

She started backing away, only to find her path blocked by what felt like an unyielding wall. Turning, she glanced at the obstacle. A shiver spread over her shoulders.

"Well," said the man directly behind her. He

smirked while his cold gaze slid over her body. "Aren't you a pretty lad."

Harriet swallowed and retreated a step. Her heart trembled. "I mean no trouble, but I do need to get on my way so I can fetch a doctor for my sister."

She wasn't sure why she said this. This man did not look the least bit sympathetic.

He chuckled. "You'll have to pay the toll first."

"The toll?"

"Aye," said one of the men who'd been standing near the end of the alley. He and the others had approached while she'd been distracted. "This is our alley. A fee's required for you to use it."

This hadn't been the case the last time she'd come this way, but a lot could change in the space of a year. St. Giles's crews could find new spots in which to fleece people by instilling fear. This was clearly such a case, which meant she'd get nowhere until she complied.

"How much?" she asked.

"Ten shillings should do it."

Harriet shook her head. "I can't afford that."

"You said you were on your way to fetch a doctor," one of the men remarked. "If you can afford to pay him then you can afford to pay us as well."

"I…"

Harriet pondered her options while glancing about, gauging her chance of escape. The men were bigger than she, so their movements might not be as agile. But was it worth the risk?

She wasn't sure, but she knew she could not afford to lose her carefully earned money to them. Not when she needed it for the doctor. Which meant she had to try and escape without losing the ten shillings they demanded.

"Fine," she said, hoping to placate them for a moment so they would let down their guards. "Ten shillings it is."

They grinned and watched as she shoved one hand in her pocket. Two of the men standing before her turned to each other, their attention briefly averted long enough for Harriet to make her move. She darted past them and raced along the length of the alleyway.

"Stop 'im!"

Harriet quickened her speed. The soles of her shoes thudded against the ground. Behind her, she could hear the men in pursuit, cursing as they ran to catch her. The exit from the alleyway wasn't far now. Just a few yards and—

A hand latched onto her shoulder, jolting her backward with such impressive force her legs tangled together. She fell, barely managing to reach her arms out in order to break the fall before she hit the ground. A jarring pain shot through her palms and knees. There was no time for her to adjust to the feeling before she was hauled to her feet and shoved up against a wall.

A large hand circled her throat and the man who'd initially blocked her path leaned in, so close she could see every piece of stubble along the edge of his jaw. "Thought ye'd cheat us, aye?"

"No," Harriet sputtered while gasping for breath.

"Such actions have repercussions," her captor snarled. He tightened his hold until tears welled in her eyes. "We're about to show ye what they are, ain't we lads?"

"Aye," the other pair agreed as they went for Harriet's pockets, divesting them of their contents while she kicked and did what she could to wrestle the strong hold away from her neck.

The grip loosened and the man stepped back. Harriet coughed and wheezed while gulping down air.

"Two pounds and ye'd not spare as much as a quarter of that for free passage?" The man who'd been holding her sneered. "Bloody fool."

He spat on the ground, wiped his mouth with the back of his hand, and sent his fist flying, straight into Harriet's jaw. The pain that followed could only be briefly ignored with each additional punch she received. Until she buckled over and dropped to her knees, sputtering as they kicked her.

She rolled to one side with a sob and hugged her stomach while blood blurred her vision.

"Do ye think ye've learned yer lesson, wee one?" the largest of the men asked while crouching so close his voice was thick in her ear.

"Yes," Harriet could barely make out the sound of her own voice it was so garbled.

The man snorted. Another kick struck her right in the back. And then she finally heard their retreating footsteps.

It took several minutes before she had the energy to push herself into a sitting position. Shaking, she stared at her hands. The knuckles were cut, her palms covered in dirt. She rubbed them on her trousers in a futile attempt to clean them, then swiped one hand across her brow to get the blood out of her eyes.

Tears rolled down her cheeks as the realization of what had transpired took hold. They'd stolen all of her hard-earned money. Four months' worth of wages. The means by which to pay the doctor. A sob fell from her lips. Despite the soreness and the occasional sting from her wounds, she pushed herself upward.

Sitting here feeling sorry for herself would not help Lucy.

Neither would returning to her lodgings empty handed. Not when all that remained there was one measly pound. No, the only options available to her now were admitting defeat or seeking help elsewhere. And as much as she loathed the idea of calling upon her friends for financial aid, she'd do it for Lucy.

Decision made, she took a deep breath, then stumbled out of the alleyway and set her course for Westcliffe House.

Brody hated being late for anything. He considered it inconsiderate to those made to wait for his arrival. But after getting to bed a little after two, he'd over-slept and didn't make it to work until ten. The note he'd received from Ramsgate requesting Finn's attendance at Hackney Meadows the following morning did little to quicken his pace.

"You should have been here two hours ago," Mr. Hudson remarked when Brody entered the office. "I've been waiting for you."

"My apologies, sir. A family matter delayed me. It won't happen again."

"I'll hold you to that and trust you won't disappoint."

"Thank you." Brody crossed to his desk and dropped his satchel next to his chair. Mr. Hudson followed him over and when Brody turned to face him, he saw that he held a manuscript in his hand. *The* manuscript. Unable to resist, Brody jutted his chin toward it. "Have you read it?"

"I have, which is part of the reason why I was so

annoyed by your late arrival. I've been waiting two hours to congratulate you on finding this brilliant novel. It's exactly what I've been hoping for – a gem of a story that's sure to delight not only Miss Austen's fans, but possibly Walter Scott's too because of the action the author has added to the plot."

Brody could not conceal his pleasure. He grinned. "That's wonderful news. I can't begin to tell you how happy I am to hear it."

Mr. Hudson gave him a curious look. "I must say, I'm not accustomed to my staff being so enthusiastic about a new publishing project. It's refreshing."

"I'm thrilled to have found the sort of book you've been looking for," Brody said in an effort to explain his reaction. "It's exciting."

"That it is," Mr. Hudson smiled. "I don't suppose you'd like to present the author with the offer I wish to provide?"

"It would be an honor."

"Right then. Here it is." Mr. Hudson handed Brody a piece of paper he'd folded and sealed with the press's logo. "I'll expect you back within two hours, preferably with a signed agreement."

"I won't let you down," Brody promised. "You have my word."

"Oh, and one more thing," Mr. Hudson remarked before Brody had managed to tuck the proposal into his jacket's inside pocket. "When you return, I'd like you to write up a vacancy for a new compositor. As regrettable as it is, I fear Mr. Michaels has left us."

Brody stilled. "Why do you think that?"

"Because he always sent a note on the few occasions when he was forced to miss work. He hasn't done so this time."

"Does that not strike you as odd?" Brody asked, wondering why Harry wasn't here. It was possible any number of things had come up, but according to Mr. Hudson, not sending word would be uncharacteristic of him.

"It does," Mr. Hudson admitted. "When you were also missing, I hoped for an explanation involving the both of you, but that clearly isn't the case. So I have to consider my business. If Mr. Michaels has been incapacitated in some way, I'll still require a new compositor. Waiting will only lead to printing delays, which is something I cannot afford for any reason."

Brody understood, but that didn't ease his concern. "If you can spare me a little while longer, I can stop by his home on my way back. Maybe he's fallen ill and failed to find a messenger who could deliver a note."

"You know where he lives?" Mr. Hudson asked in surprise.

"No. Don't you?"

Mr. Hudson shook his head. "No one here does."

"Not even Mr. Tomkins?"

"I already asked, but he says that although he has walked with Harry a few times on their way home, he's never stopped by his actual lodgings."

In other words, Mr. Michaels had vanished with little chance of being found unless he decided to show up again. The idea was shockingly bothersome and unwelcome. It filled Brody with deep disappointment as he headed for Westcliffe House.

CHAPTER TEN

Everything hurt and it felt as though Westcliffe House were hundreds of miles away. Harriet paused for a moment to gather her strength while leaning against a lamp post. Pedestrians passing by added distance, staring at her as though she were a spectacle.

By the time she arrived at her friend's Mayfair residence, she was so exhausted she feared she'd never get up once she sat. Ignoring the front door entrance, she descended the stairs to the kitchen door. There, she knocked and waited until a maid arrived.

"Yes?" The young woman gave her an apprehensive look.

"I'm here to see the duchess." When the maid shook her head and began backing away, Harriet told her, "Please let her know Mr. Harry Michaels needs her assistance. She'll—"

"Sorry, but the duchess isn't at home." The door was promptly shut and bolted. Through the glass, Harriet could see the maid eyeing her with unease before dashing away to the kitchen.

Harriet sighed. She should have expected this based on her appearance. Had she been the maid she might have responded with equal concern if a bloodied individual arrived on the doorstep. Nevertheless, she had to find a way into the house – some means by which to gain Ada's attention.

She returned to the pavement and glanced toward the front door. A familiar figure stood there, his back toward her as he used the knocker.

"Mr. Evans?"

He turned at the sound of her voice. His eyebrows shot toward his hairline as his mouth fell open and his eyes widened.

"Mr. Michaels?" Abandoning the knocker, he ran down the steps and was instantly at her side. "Where have you been and what on earth happened to you?"

Harriet swallowed past the dryness in her throat. "I had an unfortunate run-in with some thugs."

He grabbed her upper arm. His expression darkened. "Where?"

"A couple of miles back." She ignored the disapproving look she received from a pair of well-dressed ladies as they strolled by. "They'll be long gone by now, I should think."

"Too bad," Mr. Evans said, his voice low and rough. "I'd have enjoyed giving them what they deserved for treating you thus."

"It's fine. That is, I've more important matters to think of, which is why I came here." She stared at him while acknowledging his sharp appearance. "Are you acquainted with the duke and duchess or are you running an errand on Mr. Hudson's behalf?"

"I, um…" He scratched the back of his neck and prepared to say something more when the front door to Westcliffe House opened.

A man, all dressed in black save for his white cravat, appeared. He stared at Mr. Evans, then at Harriet, then at Mr. Evans once more. "Your—"

"I'd like to see the duke, if he's available," Mr. Evans interrupted.

"Of course," said the butler. "Do come in."

"Do you wish to accompany me?" Mr. Evans asked Harriet.

"Yes. I need to speak with the duchess."

Mr. Evans held Harriet's gaze for a long awkward moment before he eventually gestured for her to precede him inside.

"My friend will be joining me," he informed the butler when the man appeared on the verge of protesting.

"Very good, Your—"

"Thank you," Mr. Evans quipped, cutting the butler off once more.

Harriet frowned. Something about Mr. Evans's behavior was most unusual, though she could not for the life of her put her finger on what it might be. She entered the beautiful foyer where intricate crown molding graced the ceilings and white marble floors gleamed as though newly polished. Plush red runners softened their footfalls as they walked to the parlor.

"Would the young sir like a bowl of water in which to wash his hands?" The butler inquired. "Perhaps a towel for his face?"

"Thank you. That would be much appreciated," Harriet told him.

"Excellent. I'll have a maid bring you the items while I inform the duke and duchess of your arrival."

The butler vanished and Harriet breathed a sigh of relief. The tension building inside her since having her money stolen dissipated enough for her to relax. If only a little.

"You can sit if you like," Mr. Evans informed her while studying her with too much interest for her liking.

She turned her gaze away from his, choosing instead to go and admire the street view. "My clothes are filthy. It would be ill-bred."

"I was worried about you, you know."

The comment caused her heart to beat a little bit faster. "Really?"

"Of course. Everyone was. Mr. Hudson included."

Her shoulders slumped. "Oh."

"He said it was very unlike you to stay away from work without sending word of your absence." A pause followed and when Harriet said nothing further he asked, "So will you tell me what happened?"

"My sister's sick. I need to fetch a doctor for her."

"And this brought you here?"

"It was the only place I could think to go," Harriet told him wearily.

He said nothing to this and a silence ensued for a while before he suddenly asked, "How do you know the duchess?"

"It's…er…"

Thankfully the maid arrived in that instant, enabling Harriet to avoid the question. The young woman she'd met before at the kitchen entrance nearly dropped her tray. "You're here?"

"Yes." Harriet sent her a smile. "I'm sorry if my appearance put you on edge before. Thank you for bringing these things so I can clean up a little."

"You're welcome." She set the tray on the table closest to where Harriet stood and bobbed a quick curtsey before retreating with hurried steps.

Harriet dipped her hands in the bowl of water and watched it turn a grimy shade of pink.

"Well?" Mr. Evans pressed. "I'm genuinely curious to know."

"Know what?" Harriet asked as she dipped the corner of the towel she'd been brought into the washbowl so she could dab at her face. She hissed in response to the sharp sting.

"How are you, a compositor, well enough acquainted with a duchess to call upon her at her home?"

"I knew her before she married," Harriet said, doing her best to appease his curiosity with just enough information for her presence in Westcliffe House to make sense. "Her uncle owns a bookshop and often orders from Hudson & Co. I met Her Grace during some of my deliveries. The two of us became friends."

"Really?" There was an edge to Mr. Evans's voice now that made Harriet slightly more uncomfortable. "And that's all there is to it?"

"Of course. What else would there be?"

"I don't know. You're a handsome young man, roughly her age. It wouldn't be strange if you'd taken a fancy to her. I simply want to make sure—"

"I promise you I have not," Harriet said with a laugh.

"All I'm saying is that the duke is *my* friend. I'd hate to think you might pose a threat to his marriage by showing up here."

"No. I…" Harriet dropped the towel she'd been

using and frowned as she met Mr. Evans's gaze once more. "Tell me, how does an assistant editor get to be friends with a duke? One wouldn't imagine you run in the same circles."

"It's complicated." His shuttered expression informed her that she had touched on a subject he'd like to avoid, which piqued her curiosity immensely. There was definitely a story here.

"Complicated oftentimes equals interesting," she said, enjoying the wariness with which he eyed her. It was rather satisfying, having him sit in the inter-rogation chair for a change and watching him squirm. "Of course, there's a chance you're not really friends and that Mr. Hudson sent you here instead. It's working hours, after all. So maybe the duke has written a book that he plans to publish. Anony-mously, of course."

"It's not really something I want to discuss at the moment." Mr. Evans glanced at the door and looked visibly relieved when it opened and Ada arrived.

"Your Grace," said Mr. Evans. "I hope you'll forgive the intrusion but there's a matter I'd like to discuss with your husband. Also, this young man – a colleague of mine – wishes to speak with you."

The brief display of shock on Ada's face could not be denied, though she quickly hid it beneath the concern she showed Harriet. "Dear me. What's happened?"

"Lucy's sick," Harriet explained. "She's casting up

her accounts and it feels like she has a fever. I went to fetch the doctor, but got robbed on the way. The only solution that came to mind was you. I'm sorry. I wouldn't be here if I weren't desperate, but—"

"Why didn't you just return home and fetch some more money?" Mr. Evans asked.

Harriet narrowed her gaze on him. "Because there wasn't enough left. A decent doctor costs at least two pounds for the trouble. I took that with me, leaving one pound behind as savings."

"That's all you have available to you?" Mr. Evans asked, his voice incredulous.

"It's more than what I'd have managed to save if I worked one of the other jobs available to someone without a high education." She sniffed as her worry for Lucy, the beating she'd suffered, and the scrutiny Mr. Evans subjected her to collided. Her eyes started to burn so she turned away sharply and gave them a swipe, refusing to let him see her cry.

"You did the right thing," Ada said. "I'm glad you thought to call upon me for assistance."

The sound of footsteps announced the duke's arrival. He greeted Mr. Evans with his given name, which only made Harriet all the more curious about their relationship. Turning, she faced the duke at the same time as he swept his gray gaze in her direction. "Who are you?"

"Mr. Michaels."

The duke's eyebrows dipped. "And?"

"He's a friend," Ada said, saving Harriet from elaborating further.

The duke stared at Harriet, scrutinizing her until she was forced to shift her position in order to dispel the jittery feeling wreaking havoc on her nerves. "How do you know him?"

"From the bookshop," Ada told him without batting an eyelash.

He dropped her a sideways glance. "And now he's here, in our home, looking as though he's been beaten within an inch of his life. I do wonder why he decided to turn to *you* in his hour of need."

"As I said, he's a friend."

"If there's a history between you two," the duke said, "now would be the time to tell me."

Ada sighed. She sent Harriet an apologetic look, then grabbed her husband by the arm and steered him toward the other end of the room. Once there, she whispered something in his ear, in response to which his expression changed. He appeared to relax and even began to smile.

"I see." The duke straightened and returned to where he'd been standing before. He then told Harriet, "You're most welcome, Mr. Michaels. My wife and I will help you as best we can."

"Thank you, Your Grace." Harriet nearly bobbed a curtsey but caught herself at the last moment. She gave a short bow instead. "I'm indebted to you."

"Nonsense," said the duke. "The best friends help

one another without expecting anything in return. Ada, would you please give Mr. Michaels the funds he requires? I'm sure he's eager to get home to his sister."

"Of course." Ada turned toward the door. "Please come with me, Mr. Michaels."

Wincing despite her attempt at hiding her pain, Harriet followed Ada into the hallway and pulled the door shut behind her.

"I doubt I'll be able to attend the book club meeting tomorrow," Harriet said. "Will you please apologize to Emily on my behalf?"

"Of course." Ada gave her a gentle smile. "You mustn't trouble yourself. Emily will understand and if you need additional help, I'm sure she'll be happy to do what she can to offer assistance."

Harriet thanked her and waited while Ada retrieved her reticule.

"Wait here a moment," Ada said after rummaging through it. "I need to fetch a few more coins from the study."

Harriet nodded and gave her attention to the paintings on the wall while Ada hastened away. She'd always loved art. Some of her fondest memories were of watching her mother draw and of the two of them admiring the paintings in her childhood home together.

She glanced over her shoulder when she sensed someone approaching, thinking it might be Ada.

Instead it was the butler. He entered the parlor. When he returned to the hallway a couple of seconds later, he moved as though he intended to go and complete a task. Instead, he seemed to catch himself and slowly gave her his full attention.

"I understand you were turned away at the kitchen door when you first arrived. A slight, for which I'd like to express my sincerest apologies."

"Thank you, but it's quite all right. I understand why the maid who met me responded the way she did." Harriet added a self-deprecating laugh. "I do not look my best at the moment."

The butler merely dipped his head in acknowledgement of the remark. "Thankfully His Grace was able to clarify matters."

"Yes," Harriet agreed, although she rather felt it was his wife who'd done so.

"Had he not arrived at the same time as you, I fear I too would have sent you away." He gave a curt bow. "Good day, Mr. Michaels. I pray the remainder of it will be better for you."

Lips parted in shock, Harriet stared after his retreating form. He'd referred to Mr. Evans as 'His Grace'. Why would he do that unless… She shook her head, unable to grasp what she already knew to be true. It explained his smart appearance that first time she'd bumped into him on the street, though it didn't explain his position at Hudson & Co. Why on earth would a duke choose to work for a living when he didn't have to?

"Here we are," said Ada when she returned. "I'm giving you four pounds to be sure."

"It's too much," Harriet complained.

"Not when you're in dire straits." When Harriet still refused to take the money, Ada said, "Give me back whatever's left if you like, but at least you'll have it available to you, should the need arise."

Harriet flung her arms around her friend and hugged her tight. "Thank you. I've no idea what I'd have done without you."

"Called on Emily?" Ada suggested with a wry grin.

"Probably," Harriet agreed.

"You ought to head straight home from here so you can be with Lucy. I'll see to it that the doctor shows up."

"Thank you." She exited Ada's home while telling her friend, "I still can't believe you're a duchess. Or that there are currently two dukes in your parlor."

"I know, it's rather…" Ada sucked in a breath. "I don't think you're supposed to know that."

"Know what? That Mr. Evans is a duke in disguise?" She held Ada's gaze. "What's his title?"

Ada shook her head before sending a quick glance over her shoulder. "You should ask him. But before you do, you might want to consider the fact that he's not the only one pretending to be someone else. How would you feel if he worked out your secret?"

"Point taken," Harriet said. She thanked Ada once more and made her way back to her lodgings in order to check on Lucy, all the while acutely aware of the fact that Mr. Evans was so much more than the working-class gentleman she was starting to fall for. He was a duke, which placed him on an entirely different level, so far removed from her own he might as well be on the moon.

CHAPTER ELEVEN

"I trust Mr. Michaels is a friend of yours," Anthony said while Ada poured them all a cup of tea from the pot a maid had delivered. "Mathis tells me you arrived together and that you vouched for him."

"We're colleagues," Brody informed him, choosing to say as little as possible on the subject.

"Interesting coincidence, him being a friend of Ada's and you being a longtime friend of mine." Anthony smirked and for some absurd reason his eyes also danced with mischief.

"I suppose so," Brody agreed. He sipped the tea Ada handed him and noted the warning glance she sent her husband. It very much felt as though there was a secret joke he wasn't in on – or worse, that he was the brunt of.

"And what do you think?" Anthony asked.

"Of what?"

"Of Mr. Michaels, of course, what else?"

"Er…" Brody could feel his face starting to heat. Not good. The last thing he needed was for his friend to suspect something might be amiss.

He fought the urge to tug at his cravat. Hell, he'd barely allowed himself to recognize that he might find Mr. Michaels a little attractive. Not that he'd ever pursue a relationship with a man. He couldn't even wrap his head around how such a thing might work. The mechanics of it did not appeal in the slightest, but when he looked at that mouth and gazed into those hazel eyes, he had the most urgent compulsion to kiss him.

Madness. That's all this was. It would surely pass if he set his sights on a beautiful woman.

He cleared his throat. "He's very skilled at what he does. Granted, my knowledge of printing and what it involves was lacking before I began working at Hudson & Co. Having seen Mr. Michaels in action though, I believe he might be the best compositor in the country."

"He's worked very hard to hone his skills," Ada said. "Thankfully, he enjoys it, and the pay is better than most other places available to him."

"So he says." Brody drummed his fingers on the armrest. He wanted to know more about the young man but feared additional questions might be suspicious. Clearing his throat, he decided to change the subject. "I've brought some exciting news."

Anthony stilled. "Really?"

Brody grinned. "I managed to get Mr. Hudson to read our book, and he loves it. Sent me here himself for the purpose of making an offer."

Ada clapped her hands together while Anthony slapped his thigh. "Brilliant, Brody. Well done."

"I've brought the agreement with me. Mr. Hudson asked that I get it signed right away, so the only question now is whose signature we'll use." When Anthony and Ada exchanged a look, Brody said, "I'm of the opinion that Ada should be the face of the author, as initially agreed, while Anthony, Callum, and I remain anonymous."

"What say you, Ada?" Anthony asked.

"It's fine with me as long as the three of you agree to do all additional writing. But what about Callum? Shouldn't we get his opinion on this?"

"I'm certain he will agree," Brody said, to which Anthony nodded. "And if he doesn't, we'll cite a two-to-one vote."

He reached inside his jacket pocket and retrieved the agreement Mr. Hudson had prepared. Using his finger, he broke the seal and unfolded the papers. Elation poured through him when he saw the offer. He could scarcely credit it, but the sum clearly meant Mr. Hudson was very determined. He did not want the author to take the book elsewhere.

"What is it?" Anthony asked, his voice low.

Brody glanced at his friend, then at Ada, before returning his gaze to the paper he held between his hands. "We'll receive an initial advance of eight hundred pounds, to be gradually paid off with the sale of each book. After that, we'll collect thirty percent of each copy sold."

"Astonishing," Ada murmured.

"The initial print run will consist of five thousand copies and will be marketed as a grand romance for anyone fond of Jane Austen."

"How utterly marvelous," Anthony said. "Eight hundred pounds split between us will certainly help us back on our feet."

"Especially since it's payable upon completion of this contract," said Brody. He handed the agreement to Anthony so he could review it as well.

"It looks acceptable to me." He gave it to Ada.

"Shall I sign it then?"

"Please do," Anthony told her as soon as Brody gave a nod of approval.

She crossed to the small escritoire that stood against one wall and took a seat behind it.

"There's something else I probably ought to mention," Brody told Anthony. "It's personal in nature and involves my brother. Turns out he was seen kissing Ramsgate's daughter in public the night before last. Ramsgate stopped by out of courtesy to let me know he's challenged Finn to a duel. It's set to take place tomorrow morning."

"Of all the…" Anthony trailed off and eventually huffed a breath. "I'm sorry, Brody. Is there anything I can do?"

"I don't think so, unless you can come up with some way for him to avoid the altercation altogether."

"The only way to do that would be for him to marry the chit or if you can somehow convince the marquess to renege."

"I already tried that but he's determined to go through with it and marriage is off the table. Ramsgate doesn't consider Finn worthy."

"In that case, I see no other way out. If Finn himself chooses to walk away, he'll be considered dishonorable, which may not be a fate worse than death to him, but it will have a negative impact on his reputation. Forever."

"I know. I was hoping you'd have an inspired idea."

"Sorry," Anthony muttered.

His wife returned with the signed document, and Brody gave it a quick once over before slipping it into his jacket pocket. He stood and prepared to take his leave.

"You're welcome to stay for luncheon if you like," Anthony told him.

"Thank you, but Mr. Hudson gave me two hours

to handle this and check on Mr. Evans. I'm afraid luncheon would take too long."

"Of course," Anthony said. "But you still have time to check on Mr. Evans, if you wish."

"I'm not sure I need to any more. Now that I know he's all right, I can tell Mr. Hudson that he'll return to work soon."

"When do you suppose that might be?" Anthony asked. When Brody shrugged, his friend said, "We've just signed a publishing deal. It would be prudent to make sure the person charged with printing our book is capable."

"Mr. Hudson will find someone else if he isn't."

"You said yourself that Mr. Michaels is the best."

"He is."

"Well then, it stands to good reason that you should check on him, Brody. Those wounds looked like they could do with more cleaning than what was accomplished here. And if Mr. Michaels is busy taking care of his sister, he may not think to take proper care of himself."

"I'm sure he'll be fine," Ada said.

"But the wounds could get infected," Brody muttered. "His hands…"

"Not good news for a compositor I'd imagine," Anthony said.

"You're absolutely right." Why the hell hadn't he thought of this himself? Mr. Michaels depended on his hands. If the wounds weren't properly cleaned he could risk losing a finger, possibly more.

Good God.

"By the way, Ada," Anthony said while all sorts of horrid scenarios swam through Brody's brain. "Did you send one of the footmen to fetch the doctor?"

"I did."

"Very good. I do believe Brody will meet him at Mr. Michaels's home. If you could please provide the address."

"Honestly, Anthony, I'm not sure that's—"

"Trust me, Ada." He leaned in and kissed her cheek in a show of affection that instantly made Brody long for that sort of connection with the right woman. Infuriatingly, the face he envisioned when thinking of kissing was Mr. Michaels's.

Ugh!

Much to Brody's surprise, Ada rolled her eyes and shook her head with bemusement. She finally gave up the address as though she believed it to be the sort of idea that was bound to land them all in a great deal of trouble.

Brody didn't understand it. If Mr. Michaels was her friend, surely she would appreciate Anthony's reasoning. It made perfect sense to Brody. Checking on Mr. Michaels was without doubt the correct thing to do. It was certainly the only way for him to have a clear conscience.

CHAPTER TWELVE

Harriet had barely returned home before someone knocked on the door. She glanced at her sister who thankfully slept. Her temperature was still high and the bucket Harriet had cleaned before heading out three hours ago had since been used. As had the chamber pot.

"Coming," Harriet shouted when additional knocks landed against the door.

She rushed to the window and pushed it open, hoping to rid the room of some of the stench before admitting the doctor.

Aware that she herself looked a mess, she crossed to the door, unlocked it, and pulled it open. Instead of the sweet relief she'd expected to feel however, she was horrified to discover Mr. Evans. Who wasn't Mr. Evans at all. He was a duke and he presently stood on the threshold of what she could only describe as a hovel compared with what he was probably used to.

"Ah…" Her voice caught in her throat.

"Shall we proceed?" Someone spoke from behind Mr. Evans. He would remain Mr. Evans until she learned his title. As it turned out, the doctor was hidden behind his tall frame.

"Well, Mr. Michaels?" Mr. Evans raised an eyebrow and waited.

All Harriet could think to say was, "You're not supposed to be here."

She did step aside however, not to grant Mr. Evans admittance but so the doctor could enter.

He glanced at her as he stepped through the door and drew to a halt, his studious gaze searching her face before sweeping over the rest of her. "Looks like you could do with some medical attention too."

"I'm fine," Harriet muttered, earning a frown from the doctor. "My sister's the one who requires your help."

Dismissing the duke in her shabby lodgings for just one moment, she gestured toward the cot where Lucy lay. In doing so, her gaze landed upon the bucket of vomit and the chamber pot she'd not yet managed to empty.

Her eyes widened as she quickly ran to shove both items out of sight. The doctor was used to seeing such things and besides, his opinion didn't matter. But the duke?

Harriet cringed and took a deep breath, her nose instantly scrunching as she was met by the foul odor filling the room. It would take a while for the open window to take effect.

"She's certainly hot, that's for sure," said the doctor. "I'll need that bucket of puke you hid along with the chamber pot."

Lord have mercy. Where was that hole she longed to disappear into?

Accepting defeat and utter humiliation, she collected the items and set them before the doctor so he could examine both. He grunted, gave a satisfied nod, and returned his attention to Lucy.

"Ah, you're awake," said the doctor. "I'm Doctor Fielding. I've come to see if I can discern the cause of your ailment. Tell me, does anything pain you right now?"

"My stomach," Lucy moaned. "Feels like glass."

"May I?" He reached out as though meaning to touch her, and waited until she gave her consent.

Harriet glanced at Mr. Evans, whose attention was fixed on the doctor's movements with such intensity it almost looked like he willed him to make Lucy better. And in that moment, Harriet's heart expanded. She'd thought she might be falling for him before, but no. That had been nothing more than physical attraction while this…this was falling. Knowing he cared, not only for her but for her sister, instilled in her a deep emotion akin to having found her way home.

To him.

It terrified her beyond measure.

Sensing her gaze, he glanced toward her and offered a tender smile – the sort that pierced her soul while binding her to him with added force. She attempted a smile of her own, then returned her attention to the doctor who currently pressed down on the lower right side of Lucy's stomach.

"Does it hurt right here?" the doctor asked.

Lucy shook her head. "It's more to the middle."

The doctor straightened. "I don't believe it's anything too severe. The vomit isn't milky as it would be with cholera. Based on her symptoms, however, I do believe it's related to something she ate or drank."

"But we've had the same food," Harriet said

"What about when you're not home?" Mr. Evans quietly asked.

Harriet shook her head. "I usually leave her some bread along with some ham and cheese. Or a pie from the baker's. That's what she had yesterday, but I had the same when I returned home and I'm fine."

"It's possible someone handling the food was sick and passed it on. You might just be more resilient."

The doctor glanced at Lucy. "I recommend she gets plenty of fluids and that her meals for the next two days are as basic as possible. A slice of toast with butter or some porridge will do."

"Thank you, Doctor."

Straightening, he studied her before saying, "Those cuts on your hands and face need tending. If you like, I can help."

"That won't be necessary." She'd no intention of spending extra money on having a doctor clean her wounds. Besides, she was rather eager to get both men out the door.

With that in mind, she prepared herself for the most dreaded part of this conversation. For though she believed she had enough funds to cover the cost, she was determined to repay her friend. The higher the sum, the longer that would take. She took a deep breath. "How much do I owe you?"

The doctor glanced around, allowing his gaze to slide over the room while Harriet scrunched her toes. "Will ten shillings do?"

Her jaw dropped. "But that's…that's…" Less than a quarter of what she'd expect. "Are you certain?"

"Quite."

"Thank you, sir." Lord, she could barely get the words past the sudden knot in her throat. She dug her hand into her pocket and retrieved some of the coins Ada had lent her. After counting out the correct sum, she handed it to the doctor. "Your help is much appreciated. Thank you once again."

The doctor gave her a solid nod, told her to call on him if her sister's condition worsened, and left.

Harriet turned, acutely aware of the large man crowding the room. His piercing blue eyes were fixed on her with quiet interest.

It took some effort suppressing the shiver that stole down her spine. "Why did you come here?"

"To make sure you're all right." The low timbre with which he spoke vibrated through her.

Her pulse quickened. "Thank you, but I'll be fine. You should probably get back to work."

"I will, once I've checked on your wounds."

"What?" He was approaching with a very determined expression. Harriet took a step back. "There's no need for that. I already told the doctor I'm fine."

"I beg to differ."

He took both her hands in his, bringing their difference in size into focus. Harriet struggled to breathe. Goodness, she couldn't even swallow. Her throat was too tight. The feel of his fingers exploring her wounds with the utmost of care turned her legs to jelly. Her stomach flipped and her face felt alarmingly hot.

And then he raised his hand. His fingertips grazed her brow. And it was as if she'd been pushed off a cliff. Her world spun while she fell and her gaze snapped to his. He was watching her closely – too closely – his attention upon...her mouth?

No. That couldn't be. Surely she must be mistaken. He was merely assessing her wounds. Right?

Yet she sensed the air shift between them. The atmosphere had somehow thickened and her muscles were suddenly clenching in anticipation of change.

With a gasp, she withdrew and retreated from him. "I think I can manage."

His answering smile was soft and warm. "Are you certain?"

"Very much so. Yes."

He inclined his head while studying her. He eventually nodded, his features suddenly grave. "I'll respect your wishes, but I expect you to have those wounds properly cleaned."

"Of course." Needing something with which to busy herself, she went to collect a bowl and fill it with water. "If you could please let Mr. Hudson know I'll be back at work tomorrow, I'd appreciate it."

"Of course." He didn't move. "Would you like me to help you clean up before I go?"

When she glanced at him, he jutted his chin toward the bucket and chamber pot Lucy had used. Embarrassment filled Harriet all over again. "Absolutely not."

"It wouldn't be any trouble at all. And since you're wounded, I thought—"

"Thank you, but no. I can manage."

"In that case…" He scratched the back of his head while she took a seat at the table and started tending her wounds with greater care than what she'd managed at Westcliffe House. Hopefully he'd take it as a cue for him to leave. She thanked her lucky stars when he moved to the door. "I'll see you later then, I suppose."

"Yes. Enjoy the rest of your day."

He must have sensed there was no reason left for him to stay, for he opened the door, hesitated briefly, and finally departed. Harriet held her breath for a second before she expelled it with a loud sigh. She stared at the door. Was it possible Mr. Evans had the same inclinations as Oliver?

It seemed unlikely. What were the chances of her knowing two such individuals and having both press their advances? Besides, Mr. Evans had spoken to her about bedding women and had offered advice on how to avoid contracting some horrid disease.

She shuddered and gave her attention back to her hands. One of the wounds was especially deep and required extra scrubbing. She winced as she took care of it, but her thoughts remained on Mr. Evans. Could she have misjudged the situation? The way he'd touched her and the fierce look in his eyes – the manner in which she herself had responded – had warned her that he'd meant to kiss her. As Oliver had.

She sighed. Perhaps she should have let him instead of stepping away. The trouble was that as much as she longed to feel his mouth against hers, she wanted him to be kissing Harriet, not Harry.

Bloody brilliant. I don't just fall for a man out of reach but for one who might not like women.

With a groan, she dried her hands, dipped the cloth she'd been using in water, and went to stand before the small mirror that hung from a nail on the wall. Goodness, she looked a fright. There was a cut on her brow, her cheek was bruised, and blood had been smeared across her forehead. Her upper lip was also swollen. Maybe that was why it had caught Mr. Evans's attention. Maybe she'd read the situation wrong and all he'd actually wanted to do was offer assistance.

Lord help her if she knew. Her experience with men was presently limited to the one she'd had with Oliver. Annoyed with how complicated her life had become, she swiped at her wounds. With swift movements she cleaned away the blood until she looked slightly more presentable.

She glanced at Lucy, who'd fallen into a peaceful sleep after the doctor's departure. Crossing to the bucket, Harriet picked it up and carried it from the room. She'd clean this first and then see to the chamber pot after. If luck was on her side, Mr. Evans would suffer a stroke of amnesia and forget all about her poor living conditions and the fact that she very much feared she may have looked like she would welcome that kiss.

CHAPTER THIRTEEN

When Brody arrived back at Hudson & Co., he went straight to his employer and handed him the agreement Ada had signed.

"The author accepted the offer," he said. "I was asked to give you her thanks."

Mr. Hudson beamed. "That's excellent news indeed. I can't wait to get started. Which brings me to the problem regarding Mr. Michaels.

"I managed to locate him," Brody said. "His sister is sick and required attention. He apologizes for not sending word, but it's my belief his morning was spent locating a doctor. In any event, he has assured me that he will return to work tomorrow morning."

"Very good. Thank you, Mr. Evans. That certainly is welcome news since I very much want a man of his skill to be working on this new project."

"I couldn't agree with you more," Brody said. "If you like, I can inform the print room."

"Yes, yes." Mr. Hudson, his attention already back on the manuscript he'd been perusing when Brody arrived, waved him off.

Brody strode to the print room where he found the men Mr. Michaels worked with sweeping the floor and tidying the shelves. The tempo had certainly slowed since he'd been here last.

He entered the room and cleared his throat to attract their attention. "I've come to inform you that Mr. Michaels will be joining you again tomorrow."

"Is he all right?" asked Mr. Tomkins, who did the reading for Mr. Michaels.

Brody explained the situation while the three men looked appropriately concerned. He chose not to mention the attack on Mr. Michaels, deciding this was more personal in nature and that the young man could reveal as much or as little as he chose himself.

"Is there anything I can help you with here in the meantime?" Brody asked.

"I don't suppose you're able to read while I set some type?" Mr. Tomkins said. "I'm not as quick as Mr. Michaels, but we've only got three pages left of the chapter we're working on, which shouldn't take long. It would be nice if we could finish before he returns."

"I'm happy to give it a try," Brody said, "provided

Mr. Hudson has nothing else for me to do. I'll check with him and let you know."

When Brody returned five minutes later with Mr. Hudson's consent, he perched on the stool he'd seen Mr. Tomkins use and accepted the page that was handed to him.

"Read from there, one sentence at a time," Mr. Tomkins said. "I'll let you know when to continue."

Brody did as he asked, allowing the print room to get back to work. It was, in truth, a welcome distraction. During his walk from Mr. Michaels's lodgings, Brody had thought of little besides the wounded young man he'd left behind. And the fact that he'd almost kissed him.

Had it not been for Mr. Michaels stepping away, he would have done so. He would have kissed him. On the mouth!

There weren't enough words in the English language to try and explain how such a thing could have happened. How it had come to this when he'd always been drawn to women? He loved their luscious curves and enjoyed the pleasure he found with them in bed. But that mouth…

It tempted him with a frightening degree of purpose. He'd not been strong enough to resist the pull. Which was perfectly mad. *He* was mad. Or at least he felt like he was since all he could think of was Mr. Michaels and what it might be like to taste those lips.

Ugh!

Enough.

He read the next sentence and savored the brief reprieve from his uneasy musings. Thankfully the rest of the chapter required four hours of work, after which Brody's admiration for those who worked the print room grew. It wasn't easy. He himself was downright exhausted. And all he'd done was sit on a stool and read. But his throat was sore and he could not wait to get home and relax in one of his plush armchairs.

First, he intended to check on Mr. Michaels though. Not because he longed to see him again or because he couldn't seem to get the man out of his mind, but because he worried. Both over him and his sister. He wanted to make sure all was well and…

He paused on a sudden idea. It could prove disastrous. With the duel between Finn and Ramsgate now scheduled for the next morning, he had enough to worry about. But the fact was Mr. Michaels's living conditions weren't the best. Least of all for a sickly child in need of recuperation. So it made sense for someone in Brody's position to offer assistance.

First, however, he'd have to convince Mr. Michaels to let him back into his room.

He knocked when he arrived roughly one hour later. And waited. The sound of rustling ensued from behind the door, along with a series of thuds. It took a while before the door was finally opened by a bleary looking Mr. Michaels. He stared at Brody with undeniable surprise before covering a yawn with his hand.

Feeling bad, Brody gave him a sheepish smile. "Sorry. Were you sleeping?"

He nodded. "Why are you back?"

"I decided to check on you and your sister once more. How are the two of you doing?"

"Lucy ate some toast a couple of hours ago. She cast up the lot and is once again sleeping. I, on the other hand, am fine despite feeling as though my body was taken apart and reassembled."

"I'm sorry. May I come in?"

"I'd rather you didn't." Mr. Michaels averted his gaze, his embarrassment clear in his pinkening cheeks.

Brody understood. He knew they were of a different class, and that Mr. Michaels was embarrassed by his inferior situation, even though Brody saw no reason why this should be. Mr. Michaels was so remarkable as an individual, he might have lived in a hole and Brody would still be impressed.

Inhaling deeply, he prepared himself for the battle ahead. "There's something I'd like to discuss. It would be easier if we can sit down together and talk it through."

Mr. Michaels' eyes widened. "Is it about work? Has Mr. Hudson sacked me?"

"No," Brody rushed to assure him. "All is well at work. In fact, I helped your team complete the chapter you were working on yesterday."

"Really?"

He nodded. "It's tough work and I was sitting down. I applaud you setting all of that type while on your feet the whole day."

"I used to have a stool, but it got in the way when I had to deliver the forms to James. Standing was more efficient."

Brody grinned. "You truly are incredible, do you know that?"

Mr. Michaels's cheeks immediately reddened and he looked adorably bashful.

Brody shook himself. "What I wish to discuss may take time, that's all. I'd rather not do it while standing out here in the stairwell where any number of people might overhear."

Apprehension filled Mr. Michaels's gaze but instead of protesting further, he stepped aside and allowed Brody to enter.

"I apologize for the lackluster surroundings," Mr. Michaels said, his voice conveying a strong degree of self-consciousness over the squalor.

"I barely noticed," Brody said, attempting to make light of the situation and put him at ease.

"Highly unlikely for someone like you, I should think."

That got his attention. "Someone like me?"

Mr. Michaels stared at him as though weighing whether or not to say more. Eventually he confessed, "I know you're a duke."

"Ah."

"Westcliffe's butler gave it away."

"Hmm…" It was Brody's turn to feel slightly embarrassed. He'd been caught in an act of deception by someone he highly admired. Then again, Mr. Michaels would have learned the truth soon enough once Brody divulged his plan. But at least he would have learned it from him instead of from Anthony's butler. He studied Mr. Michaels a moment, unable to figure out if the news bothered him or not. "Are you angry with me for lying to you?"

"Why should I be? It's not my business if you're a duke masquerading as someone from the working class, though I must confess I'm puzzled. Even if what you said about your financial troubles is true, the salary you receive at Hudson & Co. can't possibly be enough to cover a fraction of your expenses. So why do it?"

"Let's sit and I'll explain." They pulled out the two wooden chairs that stood at the table and lowered themselves into them. Brody raked one hand through his hair and began. "My father's death a few years ago made me foolish. In an effort to ignore my grief, I wasted most of my fortune on silly pursuits. Parties, gambling, and whoring, mostly. My friends did the same, having lost their fathers in the same ridiculous accident."

"I'm so sorry."

"We eventually became wiser, but by then we were bordering on financial ruin. Given our status within Society, expectations must be met. We can't just go out and get a job. The way to a peer's wealth is through inheritance and investment. Sadly, we squandered our inheritances and had terrible luck with our investments. And then Anthony – West-cliffe, that is – met your friend, Ada. She imparted some information regarding books and suggested that with Miss Austen's unfortunate death last year, a gap has appeared in the market."

Mr. Michaels nodded. "I'm actually in agreement. If a new author were to write a romance in a similar vein, I'm sure it would be torn from the shelves of every bookshop in the country."

"Precisely what Ada believed, and convinced us of it too." He held Mr. Michaels's gaze. When he spoke next, it was in a whisper. "What I'm about to tell you doesn't leave this room. You cannot breathe a word of it to another soul. Understood?"

Mr. Michaels nodded. "You can trust me."

For some incredulous reason, considering how brief their acquaintance had been, Brody didn't doubt it. Perhaps it was in Mr. Michaels's tone or the seriousness with which he seemed to approach everything he did, from work to caring for his sister. He seemed responsible. Trustworthy. And while Brody knew he was taking a risk – that the secret he was about to share was not his alone – he'd rather divulge it than have Mr. Michaels find out on his own. The chance of his doing so was certainly there, unless Brody gave him an adequate explanation for why he'd chosen to work at Hudson & Co.

The truth seemed like the best option.

"My friends and I have written a book together. A romance novel, to be precise."

Mr. Michaels's lips parted with notable surprise. "Really?"

Brody nodded and had to clasp his hands together to stop them from trembling. He was suddenly nervous. More so than he'd been at any other point in his life. It was ridiculous, but it occurred to him that Mr. Michaels's opinion on this mattered. Greatly.

Why? He could not – no, he dared not – say.

"I'm very impressed," Mr. Michaels said, prompting a surge of warmth to expand Brody's chest. "Writing a novel is no small feat. I've tried."

"You have?"

"Gave up after the second chapter when I realized how long it would take to complete the story." He shrugged. "I must not have wanted it badly enough. Or rather, I preferred reading to writing. Being part of the book creation process has always been a dream of mine though, and thankfully, opportunity gave me that chance."

"As far as I can tell the job of compositor fits you perfectly."

It was the strangest thing, but there was no doubt the compliment made Mr. Michaels blush all the way to his ears. He laughed with that sort of uncomfortable need to hide his response. The effect on Brody confirmed that he felt more for Mr. Michaels than what was proper and that his attraction toward the young man was no passing thing. However inconvenient and illegal it was.

Hell, if he pursued a relationship with him and he were discovered, his actions would see him hanged. Perhaps Mr. Michaels too. It was certainly enough to make a man think more than once or twice before acting. Wanting a kiss wasn't nearly enough to risk his life over.

But if things progressed and he grew fonder of Mr. Michaels – if his feelings for him deepened and he fell in love—what then?

Would he be willing to stake his life on having a proper relationship with him?

His heart beat with sluggish movements. The very idea of what it would mean to bed him squeezed his lungs until he struggled to breathe.

He winced. A kiss was one thing a shag quite another. His stomach roiled. Christ have mercy, if only Mr. Michaels had been born a woman.

"Mr. Evans?"

Brody blinked. "Yes?"

"Is something wrong?" Mr. Michaels was watching him with a mixture of curiosity and concern.

Giving his head a quick shake to dislodge all the muddled thoughts he'd been having, Brody folded his arms on the table. "Sorry. I got a bit distracted, that's all."

"My apologies. I shouldn't have taken control of the conversation like that. Not when you were trying to tell me something important. Please, go ahead. I'd love to know more about this project of yours."

Brody smiled. He liked the term 'project'. It fit the undertaking he and his friends had embarked on perfectly. "After several failed attempts at getting our novel published, I happened upon the announce-ment in Hudson & Co.'s window. It seemed like an excellent opportunity to get the novel noticed, so I applied for the job of assistant editor. After reviewing a few of the manuscripts in the slush pile, I finally showed the novel my friends and I had written to Mr. Hudson, who instantly loved it and asked me to present his offer to the author. That's why I was at Westcliffe House."

"Incredible." Mr. Michaels gazed at him in dismay. "You mentioned friends, as in plural. Who else besides you and Westcliffe is involved in this project?"

"The Duke of Stratton."

Astonishment filled Mr. Michaels's eyes. "It's hard to grasp. Not so much the writing part, but the fact that you're a duke is something I still can't get used to."

"I would prefer if you didn't," Brody said. "I've enjoyed being treated without any fuss."

"So I shouldn't start saying, 'Your Grace'?"

"Don't you dare."

Mr. Michaels chuckled before growing once again serious. "What's your title?"

"Corwin, but I'd rather you call me Brody."

"Brody."

Brody shifted uncomfortably in his seat. The way Mr. Michaels whispered his name was too bloody sensual. And cause for additional worry.

Bloody hell and all its demons. What a disaster.

"I suppose you should call me Harry then."

Brody nodded. Still numbed by the knowledge that everything he'd always known to be true of himself had been flipped on its head, he took a deep breath and slowly expelled it. "I'd like that. In fact, the matter I wish to discuss would probably be more acceptable to us both if we're on familiar terms. Close friends, that is."

Harry looked suddenly wary. "Go on."

Brody met Harry's gaze directly. "I want to

propose that you and your sister come stay with me at my home until she has fully recovered."

As he'd expected, Harry immediately shook his head. "Out of the question. We couldn't possibly. I mean, it wouldn't be proper."

The last part of his complaint gave Brody pause. He frowned. "I don't see why not. I've had friends visit from out of town plenty of times without it being the least bit improper. And if it's your sister you're thinking of, she would be in your care. Plus, she's too young for her presence to cause a stir with anyone, I should think."

"It's very kind of you to offer, Mr….ahem… Brody, but I really must decline." He was fidgeting with the makeshift bandage he'd wrapped around his right hand. "The last thing you need, if you're truly in financial straits, is two extra mouths to feed. Never mind the trouble of having a sickly child in your home."

"First of all, my financial straits are not as dire as all that. As for the sickly child, I'm happy to do what I can to help my friend's sister. It wouldn't be a problem at all."

"Perhaps not but—"

"Consider this before you dismiss the idea too quickly." Brody glanced at the sickly girl, his heart aching for her. He could not leave her to suffer in this wretched place when he had the means to provide her with proper care. Somehow, he had to convince her brother. "Lucy will have her own room with a comfortable bed. She'll have servants to help her during the night, so you're not exhausted for work in the morning. And she can have baths – as many as she desires. There's even a library filled with books where she can find something engaging to read should she get bored. Plus, my cook is excellent. She'll make some good soup once Lucy is ready for more than toast and porridge."

Harry gaped at Brody in silence for so long it almost looked like his brain had disconnected from his mouth. He eventually sighed. "That does sound rather lovely. I just don't feel as though you and I have been friends long enough for it not to look like I'm taking advantage."

"How can you be taking advantage when I am the one who suggested it to you?"

"I'm still not sure. I mean, this place may not be much but it's our home. It's where we have all our things."

Brody glanced around, unsure of what all these things Harry referred to might be. He decided to hold his tongue on that score. Instead he said, "I can send a trunk or two over so you can pack. Bring whatever you need."

Harry hesitated. "Are you sure?"

"Without a doubt."

Another sigh followed before Harry finally nodded. "Very well then. If you're sure we won't be a bother, we'll come for a visit. But only until Lucy is well enough to hold down food and her fever has gone."

"Perfect." He'd convince them to stay a bit longer once they got settled, but for now he'd take what he could. With this in mind, he told Harry to start preparing for his and Lucy's departure, and left with the promise that he'd be back soon with a carriage.

CHAPTER FOURTEEN

This wasn't meant to have happened.

Harriet stared in silent amazement at the parlor she'd been led to. It was just as impressive as everything else she'd seen of Corwin House so far. Crown moldings adorned every ceiling. Wainscoting graced every wall. Chandeliers dripping with crystals lit every room. The bedchambers, both hers and Lucy's, were so luxurious Harriet feared she might tarnish the space the moment she set foot inside it.

If only she had more appropriate clothes to wear.

Unfortunately, she possessed only two masculine outfits, one of which required a thorough laundering after her scuffle that morning. She'd changed into a set of clean clothes before coming here, but she still felt like a pauper who belonged more readily on the street than in such splendor.

She shouldn't, she reflected after making sure

Lucy was installed in her bedchamber and all her needs met. Before their father died, she and her sister had both been accustomed to comfortable living, though nothing quite as extravagant as this.

Standing in front of a tall window framed by curtains crafted from golden silk, Harriet gazed out at the street. Even that was expensive looking compared with where she currently resided.

"Are you sure Lucy is happy with the room she's been given?" Brody asked, pulling Harriet away from her thoughts.

She turned and considered the man who was so much more than she'd ever imagined. Not just an editor's assistant, or a duke, or even a friend, but someone with whom she sensed she could have been happy, if life had dealt them a different hand.

"It exceeded her expectations," Harriet said. "Mine too, I admit."

"I'm glad." He smiled warmly, prompting her heart into a hopeful flutter. "And you're welcome to take a bath too if you like. Dinner can wait another half hour."

"Thank you, but that would give your staff extra trouble. Besides, I thought I'd wait with my bath until I'm ready to retire." She gave him a sharp look. "Unless you've determined I need one sooner."

He laughed and crossed to the sideboard. "No. It's fine. You can wait if you like. I generally like to have my bath before bed as well. Drink?"

She'd never tasted liquor before in her life. Only wine, the ale Brody had bought her and once, a glass of champagne. Brandy wasn't something she was too keen on trying, but men did drink it, so wouldn't it make sense for her to have some after the day she'd just had?

"Please," she said, deciding that it would at least give her something to do with her hands.

They'd been fidgety ever since Brody had asked her to visit. Agreeing to do so presented her with a couple of challenges she would much rather avoid. For instance, she still had her courses and would have to hide that from Brody's maids. There were too many people here paying attention. And what if Lucy accidentally let it slip that Harriet wasn't a man? She never used the name Harry. Only Harriet.

"Here you go." Brody held a glass toward her, and as she took it, her fingers brushed his. The touch was fleeting, though just as affecting as when he'd held her hands earlier today. Sparks shot up her arms and made her skin sizzle. Her gaze instinctively darted to his and the intensity she saw there rendered her breathless.

Unable to utter one word, she shook her head while once again wondering if she imagined the raw desire she was seeing, for if she didn't…

Her stomached tightened and her knees grew weak. Brody grabbed her elbow. "All right? You looked a bit dizzy for a moment."

"It's, um…nothing. I'm fine."

"Let's hope this thing Lucy has isn't contagious."

"Yes." Her voice sounded faint and husky. Unsure of what to do with it, she clinked her glass against Brody's then sipped her drink. And promptly winced in response to the bite. The brandy was stronger than she'd expected, and now she was coughing as well. How perfectly marvelous when her intention had been to look suave.

Brody slapped her back hard. "I take it you've never had brandy before?"

"No," she sputtered. There was no point in lying.

He laughed, though not in a way that made her feel more embarrassed, but rather like someone sharing a joke with a friend. "Perhaps you should have the port instead."

"Is that milder?"

"Very much so." He prepared a glass and was just about to hand it to her when he paused, deciding to set it down on a table instead. "Give it a try."

She placed the glass to her lips, ever conscious that he kept his gaze upon her as she drank. The sweeter flavor was soothing and much more agreeable to her taste buds. "I like it."

He chuckled. "Good. Feel free to help yourself whenever you like. It's the bottle that's farthest to the right."

"Thank you. For everything. I'm in your debt."

"Don't think like that." He suddenly reached up

and brushed his fingertips over her brow. "You did well, cleaning the wound. Here too."

His fingertip brushed her lip, the hot sensation the act produced shooting straight to her core. She gasped and watched his eyes darken. Her stomach tightened and her pulse began racing. Whatever doubts she'd had about his intentions before were promptly dismissed. He lusted for Harry.

No sooner had she determined this than he dropped his hand, muttered a curse, and removed himself to the opposite side of the room. Her heart ached from the loss, not only of his touch but in knowing that he would have no interest in Harriet, just Harry.

"Sorry." He cleared his throat. "Didn't mean to make you uncomfortable there. It's quite the cut you sustained though. It's good to see that there's little chance of infection."

"Of course." It would have been a reasonable explanation had he only touched her brow, but pressing his fingertips to her lips was overstepping by leaps and bounds. Surely he knew this.

Before any more could be said on the matter the butler arrived to announce that dinner was served.

"A tray is being readied for your sister at her request," the butler informed Harriet once she was seated at the table. "I do hope that's all right, but the maid attending her said she was hungry. She asked Cook to prepare a broth and some buttered toast."

"Thank you, and yes, I'm sure that will do her good."

The meal commenced, beginning with a few tasty slices of smoked salmon garnished in dill and lemon.

Brody ate his finely sliced salmon and dill dressing in silence while cursing himself to the devil. What in blazes had he been thinking, pressing his fingertips to Harry's lips in such a provocative manner. It was beyond the pale. He'd not been thinking. Any number of servants could have walked in on him having a hard-to-explain-away moment with his friend.

Good grief, he was an idiot. The startled expression on Harry's face confirmed this. The poor lad had looked like a rabbit caught in a snare by a hungry fox.

It wasn't right.

None of this was.

He wasn't supposed to find men attractive. He never had. Not once. Until now.

The effect Harry had upon him could not be denied. He felt complete when in his company – as though he'd finally found a missing part of himself. More than that, he'd started to yearn for him so fiercely he struggled to think straight.

But that didn't mean Harry shared the attraction.

On the contrary, Brody was beginning to fear he might have misjudged the lad's blushes and the shyness with which he appeared to respond when Brody touched him. Instead of interest, it might be evidence of severe discomfort, coupled with a sense of unequal status that made him fear what might happen if he rebuffed Brody's advances.

Especially now that he knew him to be a duke.

Hating himself for potentially giving rise to such alarm, he wondered how best to address the issue. Of course, he could say nothing at all and let the incident fade with time. That would probably be the wisest. But it wouldn't diminish the awkwardness that had settled between them since his blunder.

And if there was one thing Brody wanted more than anything else, it was for Harry to feel at ease in his home. Not for him to worry that his host might make demands of a sexual nature.

Damn.

His plate was whisked away and a new one appeared. This time with roast duck and potatoes.

He glanced at Harry, who sat directly at his right. "Is the food to your liking?"

"Very much so," Harry said with a smile so wide it seemed to fill the entire room with sunshine.

Brody stared. It was impossible not to.

Catching himself, he reached for his wine and downed half the glass before saying, "I only want to make sure you're in good health and properly cared for. That's all."

"I know," Harry said once he'd swallowed the food in his mouth. "And I'm grateful, so if there's a way in which I can ever repay your kindness, do let me know."

A kiss would be a good start.

"No," Brody blurted, louder than he'd intended. Harry stilled and Brody realized he was staring at him with concern. "Sorry. It's been a long day. I didn't mean…"

"It's not too late for Lucy and me to leave if you've changed your mind about us staying over."

"She's already settled in and besides, that's the last thing I want. What I would like is for you to forget about earlier, that's all. Can you please agree to do that?"

"Of course." Harry knit his brow and glanced at the table while gently adding, "Nothing happened."

"And nothing would have, but I know I made you uncomfortable, which was not my intention at all. Please, forgive me. I'm not…" He shook his head and muttered a curse before shoving another bite of food into his mouth. He chewed the piece and chased it down with some wine. "You're my friend, Harry. I like you, and seeing your handsome face cut and bruised disturbs me greatly. Hell, I'd like nothing better than to chase down those who did that to you and beat them until they're screaming for mercy. I'm sorry if my show of compassion was inappropriate. I wasn't thinking straight."

"I understand," Harry said, his words slow and measured. "You were distracted by the wounds. I believe I would have been too, had our roles been reversed."

He was saving him, Brody realized, by supporting the notion that what had transpired was perfectly normal. It hadn't been. Brody knew he'd crossed the line, and he was a hundred percent sure Harry knew this as well. But his willingness to play along was not only evidence of his friendship, but proved that he cared about Brody's feelings. It also showed how kind and good-natured Harry was. Another, less compassionate man, would have shamed Brody for his behavior before informing the world that the Duke of Corwin had made advances.

But not Harry. No, Harry was goodness personified. Hard working, dedicated, and loyal. There was nothing about him that warranted even a single complaint. Nothing Brody could think of at any rate.

Raising his gaze, he looked across the table, his heart lurching when his gaze caught Harry's.

"Thank you," was all he could manage. The feeling in his chest was too intense for him to say anything more. It was as though his heart was expanding, pressing against his ribs with such intense longing it actually pained him.

"For what?" Harry asked with a wry smile. "If

anything, it is I who ought to thank you for inviting me into your home. It's magnificent by the way."

"You like it?"

"How can I not when I've never seen anything to compare?"

"You've been inside Westcliffe House."

"Only in the parlor. While lovely, it's not as fine as yours."

Brody grinned and sat a bit straighter. It was ridiculous how pleased he was to receive such praise from Harry.

"You're welcome to roam about as you please. The music room might appeal if you play."

A wistful look caught Harry's eye. "I used to, but it's a long time ago. I'm sure I've forgotten how."

"You may be out of practice, but I doubt you would have completely forgotten." He glanced at Harry's hand, at the elegant fingers gracefully holding the wine glass. No wonder he was so good at setting type. If he played the pianoforte, his fingers would have a certain dexterity that surely came in handy.

"Maybe I'll visit the music room tomorrow and find out."

Brody liked that idea and voiced his approval.

"Would you care for an after-dinner drink in the library?" he asked when dinner was over.

Harry yawned but nodded. "I'd like to check on Lucy first, if that's all right."

"Of course." Brody led the way out of the dining room. "I'll meet you there. It's the next door on the left."

They parted ways and Brody went to prepare two glasses of port. He set them on a table between two armchairs, studied their placement a moment, then moved them both to the table in front of the sofa. Apprehension rushed through him, quickening his pulse. Why in God's name was he so bloody nervous?

Because after everything that had happened, Harry had not retreated. Had he been alarmed by Brody's actions, surely he'd have declined the drink and fled from his presence as soon as he had the chance. But no, he'd accepted the invitation to spend more time together.

Shoving his hands into his pockets, Brody crossed to the fireplace and stared at the dancing flames. He'd shown Harry his hand and Harry was still choosing to spend additional time with him alone. Did that mean he enjoyed his friendship so much that he was prepared to ignore Brody's interest in him, or did it mean that he shared it?

He'd been visibly startled when Brody had touched his lips, but maybe that was because he'd not expected it at that moment. Lord, it was hard to read him, and this made Brody feel all the more anxious. It wasn't enough that he was dealing with new and conflicting feelings, he also had to work out what the object of his desire was thinking.

Whatever the case, it would most likely be prudent of him to move slowly and gauge his responsiveness for a while before making another blunder. Not only because a mistake on his part could ruin the precious connection they shared, but because Harry's comfort was vital. However much Brody longed to push their relationship in a certain direction, he'd not jeopardize that.

His gaze went to the glasses in front of the sofa. Perhaps insisting they sit beside one another in the narrow space was a bit too forward. Regretting the idea, he went to move the glasses back to the spot between the two armchairs, just managing to pick them up when Harry arrived.

"How's your sister?" Brody asked. Choosing to give Harry his glass while standing so he could decide on where to sit on his own, he approached and offered it to him.

"She drank her broth and ate half her toast without feeling the need to vomit again. As far as I can tell, she's not quite as warm as before."

"I'm glad to hear it. I trust she's resting again?"

"Yes." Harry took the glass Brody offered, his fingertips sliding against his in the process. A sharp inhalation followed. He took a step back. "Sorry."

"It's quite all right."

I wish you'd touch me some more.

Harry sipped his drink and Brody followed suit. "Your library is very impressive."

Brody tracked Harry with his gaze as the younger man moved around the space. He trailed his fingers along the shelves, studied the titles embossed in gold leaf on the spines, and marveled at some of the rarer volumes. Happiness swam through Brody's veins. He could not have been more delighted if Harry had kissed him.

"You're welcome to borrow whichever you like."

Harry threw him a look over his shoulder, and the sparkle of pleasure that shone in his eyes nearly brought Brody to his knees. He gripped his glass and smiled back while coming to terms with a shocking discovery that set him back on his heels. Swallowing, he moved to the sofa and carefully lowered himself to it. He needed to sit as the pure intensity of his emotions cemented within him.

He didn't just care for Harry. He'd bloody well gone and fallen in love with the lad.

CHAPTER FIFTEEN

Moving slowly, Harriet took her time perusing Brody's collection. She was acutely aware of his piercing blue gaze following her every move. Earlier during dinner, when he'd brought up the incident in the parlor, she'd done what she could to ease his concerns. Truth was, she'd wished their situation might have been different and that he'd gotten to know *her* instead of Harry.

It broke her heart, knowing he fancied a ficti-tious character she had created. Harry was an illu-sion, crafted to give her the same opportunity she would have had if she'd been born a boy. Unfortu-nately Brody, much like Oliver, was drawn to his own sex. And for some absurd reason they'd both been attracted to Harry.

She shifted her feet. It really wasn't fair. Not that she would have had a chance in hell with a duke anyway, but maybe they could have at least shared a kiss?

Now?

She stared at the book spines before her and frowned. It would be foolish of her to let such a thing happen when there could be nothing more. It would be wrong when Brody would think he was kissing a man. It would be selfish of her to let it happen. Wouldn't it?

Her heart raced. There was no doubt in her mind that the duke wanted more than Harry's friendship. And she longed for more than his, so perhaps one kiss, to appease both of their curiosities would not be so very bad?

She rolled her eyes. Of course it would. What if things got out of hand? What if they lost control and he realized she wasn't the man he thought he was kissing? Their friendship would surely be over then. Wouldn't it?

Yes, she told herself firmly. It would. And that was not the sort of risk she was prepared to take. Besides, it really wouldn't be fair of her to kiss him while pulling the wool down over his eyes. That wouldn't only be wrong, but cruel.

Expelling a sigh, she grabbed the volume that had caught her interest – *The Victim of Prejudice* – and turned away from the book case. Brody now reclined on the sofa while sipping his port. She sipped her own and made her approach.

After a brief consideration she chose the armchair adjacent to where he sat – close enough so they could talk with comfortable ease without their thighs pressing together.

His gaze, more intense than ever, stayed on her as she took her seat, angling herself so she faced him more directly. She cleared her throat and placed the book in her lap, gripping it firmly to stop her hand from trembling. The nervousness she suddenly felt was incomparable. Her stomach rolled over and butterflies started flying around it, making her feel slightly ill.

"What did you pick?" Brody asked, scooting forward in his seat.

His knee bumped hers and sparks ignited at that point of contact. An intense sense of longing swept through her. She instinctively shifted with the intention of adding some distance, but the low table at the center of the seating arrangement hampered her movements.

Her stomach tightened with sudden alertness.

Clearly she'd made a severe error in judgement by choosing to sit so near him. The space was narrower than she'd imagined, and the heat his proximity stoked in her body would soon make her melt into a pathetic puddle.

Needing to calm her nerves, she took another drink while handing him the book.

"Excellent choice," he murmured, and set it aside

on the table before them. "Would you like more port?"

She realized she'd emptied her glass. "Yes please."

The liquor had the most soothing effect. It warmed her insides, eased the tension in every muscle, and enabled her to relax in a state of wonderful languor.

Instead of taking her glass with him to the sideboard, Brody collected the bottle. He returned to his spot on the sofa, sent her a dashing smile, and refilled her glass.

She took it from him and drank some more while he followed suit, his gaze snaring hers with the intimacy of a heady caress.

The hair at the nape of her neck responded, producing the most enjoyable shiver. He stretched out his legs, his feet so close to hers it would take very little for them to touch.

Another sip of port filled her mouth. She swallowed and closed her eyes briefly while savoring the lightheaded sensation it wrought.

"I've been wondering," Brody said, his voice a low rumble that did all sorts of delicious things to her body. When Harriet looked at him next, he was once again leaning toward her, not in a menacing way, but as though with interest. "Did the advice I gave you about French letters prove useful?"

Harriet blinked. She was fairly sure she should be

appalled by the question, but her brain was too relaxed for such a response. "Um…not yet."

"Did you at least visit the apothecary as I advised?"

"No."

"Why not?" He sounded genuinely curious.

She licked her lips, set her glass aside on the table, and leaned back, moving her feet so their ankles connected. He didn't move and neither did she. It was much too nice, this intimacy that existed between them. She sighed, enjoyed the weightlessness in her bones before glancing at him. "I haven't had the need."

"I find that hard to believe," Brody muttered.

"Why?"

He shrugged. "You're in your prime. Only what, seventeen years of age?"

"Eighteen, to be precise."

"And when was the last time you bedded a woman?"

"I've not…that is…I…"

A long and uncomfortable silence followed before Brody quietly asked. "Are you saying you've never done it?"

Harriet answered without even thinking. "Yes."

"I see." The remark was very observational in nature and seemed to suggest a great deal of insight.

"You're surprised," Harriet said. Of course he would be. She was supposed to be masquerading as a man, not an unmarried woman. Hoping to shrug off what he clearly viewed as unusual behavior, she told him, "There's nothing wrong with choosing not to go whoring about."

"Of course not." He sounded affronted now. "I don't much care for whoring myself."

She sent him a sidelong look. "Good to know."

He snorted. "Generally speaking, I prefer a permanent partner, of which I've had only a few."

Annoyed with the turn the conversation had taken, Harriet couldn't refrain from asking, "And who is your lucky paramour now?"

"I haven't any, at the moment, though I am hoping that might soon change."

"Really?"

"If things turn out as I hope. Truth be told, it's a bit of a tricky situation." He chuckled with enough edginess to catch Harriet's attention. "Perhaps you can advise me?"

"I can certainly try, though with my inexperience taken into account, I doubt I'll be much use."

"All I'm after right now is that first kiss." When Harriet didn't reply he asked, "You have been kissed before, have you not?"

"Of course. Oliver…" She could have bitten her own tongue off right then and there. Not even daring to look at Brody, she stared straight ahead without seeing a thing.

"Oliver kissed you?" His voice was tighter than

before, his posture a hard block of steel. "Is that what you're telling me, Harry?"

"No. That would be wrong." She leapt to her feet. Hugging herself, she backed away, moving toward the book case and adding as much space between them as possible. "I mean…it wouldn't be right. No. It wasn't Oliver. It was…it was… Mary. That's what I meant."

Brody stood and approached her with unhurried movements. "You can be honest with me, Harry. I won't accuse you or judge you."

"Please." Her eyes welled with tears, not because of herself or what she risked losing if Brody found out she wasn't a man, but for Oliver's sake. She'd sworn she'd keep his secret safe and instead she'd revealed it to someone who had the power to have him arrested and killed. Brody was no ordinary man, he was a powerful duke. She shook her head while pressing herself against the book case. "Don't tell anyone. Promise me, Brody, I beg you."

"There's no need for that," he whispered, coming to stand before her. "Your secret is safe with me. So is Oliver's. I shan't tell a soul. You have my word."

She sagged with relief. "Thank you. I don't know what I was thinking."

"I believe the wine you had for dinner and the port you've had after may have loosened your tongue. Nothing to be ashamed of." He was standing so close she'd press up against him if she were to straighten her posture. And he was watching her with the same heated look she'd seen in the parlor. It had the most inappropriate effect on her body.

"Might I ask…are you and Oliver together? As a couple, I mean."

"No."

"Why not?" He held her gaze. "I've seen the two of you interact. You clearly get along."

She swallowed and tried to think of how best to respond, but her brain wasn't working properly. It felt like a giant wad of cotton. Eventually she settled on, "We weren't compatible."

"The kiss was not to your liking?"

She wasn't sure why his questions were making her wish he would sweep her into his arms and press his mouth to hers. It was maddening and didn't make any sense. Instead of getting all needy, she ought to be in a dead panic.

She pressed her palms into the bookcase, preventing herself from flinging her arms around his neck, and shook her head. "No."

"It happens," he murmured, his fingers suddenly at her jaw. A pulse began beating in Harriet's stomach. Her throat went dry and every nerve ending sharpened with alertness. "It simply means you haven't been kissed by the right person."

Before she could take her next breath, Brody's lips brushed against hers. Once, twice, three times. Harriet couldn't move. Every inch of her body had been set ablaze by that touch. Her stomach clenched. Fire burned in her veins while desire warred with her conscience.

"Now you know," he whispered, his breath tickling her lips. "I won't say a word about you or Oliver to anyone. How can I when I share the same inclination toward you."

"Brody, I—"

He kissed her again, this time with added pressure. Moving one hand to the side of her head, he offered support, holding her steady.

His teeth nipped at her lip until she gasped, taking their kiss to a whole new level and leaving her with little choice but to wrap her arms around his neck and hold on with all her might. It was the most improper act she'd ever engaged in. It was also incendiary and wildly seductive.

The taste of the port on his tongue was delicious. Now that she'd ventured down this path she could not get enough, so she kissed him back with equal fervor, mimicking his every move.

A throaty growl rose from his throat, vibrating through her until she was desperate for something she couldn't define.

"Bloody hell," Brody muttered against her mouth before kissing a path along her jaw. "Had I known it would be like this, I'd have given up women ages ago."

The words broke through some of Harriet's lust-filled haze. "What women?"

"I'm actually rather glad you're a virgin. That way we can learn together."

"I don't understand." He made no sense.

"I've been so damn worried and very confused, not knowing how I could feel what I did, unsure of making advances and fearing the way you'd react." He returned to her mouth and kissed her deeply, ridding her brain of all else. "I'm relieved we've finally taken this step."

He pressed his forehead to hers, his breath coming hard as he set his fingertips to her lips. "You've got the most glorious mouth. I've been dreaming of it for ages, wondering what it would be like to kiss you. And do you know what I have discovered?"

"What?" she asked, her voice but a movement of air between them.

Leaning in, he scraped her jaw with his teeth before whispering in her ear, "It's bloody amazing."

The hand at her waist loosened her shirt enough for his thumb to caress her bare skin. The slow back and forth strokes made her shiver.

"Feel good?" he asked while watching her closely.

She couldn't deny it. He'd know she was lying. "Yes."

His eyes gleamed. "You're welcome to touch me as well if you like."

Harriet's fingers twitched. Lord, she was tempted and given the situation, it would be expected. She'd already come this far. What harm could it do? This would be her only chance. Come tomorrow, she'd have to sit Brody down and explain that their kiss could not happen again.

She reached for him and hooked her fingers into his waistband. He hissed when she found the skin beneath his shirt and again when she ran her fingertips over his stomach. This was wrong. A voice at the back of her head was screaming for her to stop. But how could she when it felt so wonderfully right?

Holding her gaze, Brody pulled on her shirt, freeing it a little bit more – just enough for his whole hand to slide underneath. His palm curved against her waist, gripping her firmly, and then he kissed her hard, with such possessive force heat spiked through her limbs and made her crave more.

Was she mad, kissing a man who didn't know she was a woman?

Undoubtedly.

Except it would only be this once – just enough to avoid having regrets.

An appeasing thought until she realized his hand had crept higher while she'd been distracted. His questing fingers scraped the underside of her ribs.

Harriet froze. One more inch and he'd touch her bindings.

Panicking, she grabbed his arm to still the movement and turned her head to break the kiss. "We should stop. I ought to go check on Lucy."

"Of course. I'm sorry if I got carried away." He laughed with an underlying hint of shyness that would have stolen Harriet's heart, had it not already been his. "Turns out you're rather addictive."

"I could say the same about you." She smiled while struggling to hide the ache in her breast.

This was the last time they'd be this close. Tomorrow she'd have to add distance. It was the only way for her to stop him from learning the truth about her.

As a man who risked death in order to kiss her – a duke, no less – Harriet feared what he might do if he found out that she didn't share the same danger. There was no accounting for the lengths he might go to in order to ensure her silence if he felt betrayed. Such anger could make the noblest person a slave to irrational behavior.

So it was best this way.

Feeling her heart break, she placed her palm against his cheek and caressed it lightly. She then lifted up on her tiptoes and kissed him for the last time. "Good night, Brody. I'll see you in the morning."

He echoed her sentiment, informing her that he needed to wait for his brother to get home from his dinner with friends. "There's a matter I need to discuss with him before I retire."

"Nothing too serious, I hope."

He shook his head, but a brief flicker of pain in his eyes suggested otherwise. "The maids and footmen will see to your bath if you ring the bell pull."

"It's not too late?" she asked while tucking her shirt back into her trousers.

He glanced at the clock. It wasn't yet nine. "No. And after the day you've had, I insist you allow yourself the luxury of sinking into a tub of hot water."

"Thank you, Brody."

She moved to the door, but he spoke before she reached it, halting her strides. "I'll give our new relationship some thought until we speak next. Perhaps you can do the same. All things considered, discretion will be paramount for us both."

It was hard to speak past the sudden hoarseness in her throat. "I couldn't agree more."

She slipped out into the hallway and almost sobbed in response to the wretchedness that had replaced the pleasure he'd instilled moments ago.

Good lord, what had she done?

CHAPTER SIXTEEN

I t was hard for Brody to stop from grinning. He'd never before been so chuffed or excited. Hell, the effect Harry had wrought upon him with his wandering hands, sweet sighs of pleasure, and impassioned kisses, was more intense than what he'd experienced with any woman. Whether that was because it was Harry or because he'd not realized his preference for men until now, he'd no bloody clue.

What was certain though was that he wanted more. Lots more.

The concerns he'd had about what it might be like and whether or not he could cross certain boundaries had been forgotten. All he knew was that he was in love and that he longed to pursue an attachment with Harry. Even if that meant doing things he would have sworn on his life he'd never do two weeks ago.

What mattered was that his heart was engaged, and now that he knew Harry felt the same burning attraction, nothing would stand in his way. Of course, certain measures would have to be taken. No one could ever know what they got up to behind closed doors. Fortunately, nobody frowned at the idea of two men secluding themselves in a room together. In that regard, it would be easier than carrying on with an unmarried woman.

He pondered that thought while he refilled his glass. Perhaps he could offer Harry a job. Having let his valet go last week in an effort to cut back on spending, the position was perfectly suited to their affair.

Frowning, he dismissed the idea. Harry was fond of his position so Brody would not suggest he give that up. Although having him stay here would allow him to save on his lodgings. It would also ensure that Lucy was properly cared for during the day. And Brody only needed a valet mornings and evenings to help him dress and…undress.

The idea and where it might lead was thrilling. Grinning, Brody tossed back the last of his port and set the empty glass on the table next to Harry's.

It was an excellent plan – one he could scarcely wait to share with his soon-to-be-lover come morning. He glanced at the table where *The Victim of Prejudice* lay forgotten. Brody picked up the book and paused. Maybe he wouldn't have to wait after all. If he dropped off the book before meeting Finn, he could ask for Harry's opinion then. Maybe steal one more kiss.

Filled with excitement, he left the library, book in hand.

Not even Finn or his upcoming duel could dampen Brody's mood as he climbed the stairs with a lighter tread than usual.

He arrived in the upstairs hallway just in time to see a maid named Anne and two footmen with empty buckets, exiting Harry's room.

"I trust Mr. Michaels's bath has been readied?" he asked.

"Yes, Your Grace." Anne bobbed a quick curtsey. "He should have all that he needs."

"Thank you, Anne." Brody watched the three servants disappear into the service stairwell. With one final glance at Harry's door, Brody continued past it to his own room. He'd not barge in on his guest while he was undressing or bathing, no matter how tempting it was to do so.

Their relationship, he decided, was much too fresh for that. Worse, Harry might think him too pushy or desperate. So he determined to wait in his own bedchamber for the next twenty minutes, which was the time it took him to bathe and get dressed. There was no rush. Finn wasn't expected home until ten.

Plus, the time would give him a chance to let the

euphoria from his first kiss with Harry subside enough for him to consider his reason for meeting with Finn. The main purpose was to revise his brother's will in anticipation of the duel that would take place in... He glanced at the clock. A little under eight hours.

If only there were a way for Finn to avoid it, but no matter how much Brody'd thought on the matter, he'd not been able to find an alternative solution. Of course, he could take Finn's place. He was a better swordsman. But doing so would not only damage Finn's pride. It would also embarrass him publicly.

Besides, Finn would never agree.

Brody shoved his hands in his pockets and stared out the window. The light was dimmed to an almost unnatural glow with the setting sun dipping behind the rooftops. Darkness would settle within the next hour at most. He expelled a weary breath and shook his head sadly. It was his duty as older brother to protect Finn from harm. But it was tough to do when the idiot always seemed intent on diving head first into trouble.

The only comfort he found was in knowing that Ramsgate would not fight to kill. The duel was to first blood only, but that didn't mean a man couldn't die. Accidents happened, after all, and they were more likely to do so when men wielded deadly weapons.

He glanced at the clock and experienced some

relief at noting the hour. Harry ought to be done with his bath by now. Seeing him again, if only briefly, would be like a balm to his troubled soul.

Grabbing *The Victim of Prejudice* – his excuse, that was – he left his bedchamber and walked the short distance to Harry's. There he paused outside the door. His heart started pounding and his hand clenched the book. A sweat broke out at the nape of his neck. This was worse than the first time he'd had to ask a young lady to dance.

He'd just turned seventeen. Papa and Mama had insisted he dance. He'd been extremely self-conscious, knowing he'd not yet mastered the steps. Thankfully all had worked out in the end. His dance partner had made it easy since she'd been as clumsy as he. They'd laughed about it together, both during and after, and had always saved a dance for each other since. Even after she'd married.

He took a deep breath and expelled it.

Don't be a dunderhead, Brody. This is your house. Knock on the bloody door.

He gave it a quick rap. When nobody answered he made a second attempt. "Harry?"

Still nothing. He must have finished his bath faster than Brody expected and gone back to check on Lucy. A touch disappointed, Brody decided to drop the book off on Harry's nightstand. He tried the handle and the door swung open, allowing

Brody to enter at the exact same time as a naked body emerged from the tub.

Brody stared. Harry must have had his head underwater and been unable to hear the knocks. But even as what Brody saw made his body react with need, the information his eyes were sending his brain didn't make any sense.

"What the hell?"

Harry gasped as he turned in Brody's direction, slipping and almost falling in his attempt to cover himself. Except this wasn't Harry. It couldn't be. There were certain bits missing. Bits that should have been there if this was indeed the lad Brody had kissed.

"Can you please shut the door?" asked the person – *not* Harry – now crouching inside the tub.

Brody flinched as if struck before doing as asked and setting the book he'd brought with him aside on the dresser. He stared at the tub, unable to fathom this turn of events as he made his approach and peered inside. While his body was clearly pleased to discover the naked woman before him, his brain was beginning to take an entirely different stance.

His jaw tightened as anger and hurt began taking root. He'd been deceived in the most spectacular way possible.

"What is this?" he growled. "What's going on?"

"May I please have a towel?"

He glared at the individual he'd imagined himself

in love with. "No. I think I'll let you huddle there in discomfort for a moment – give you a chance to feel what I've felt since the moment we met. Who are you?"

"Harriet Michaels," she whispered, her voice tiny and meek, though she did hold his gaze.

"Well, I must congratulate you on your mighty success. I fell for your act in every conceivable way." He snorted. "That was your intention, was it not?"

"I'm sorry. I never meant for things to get out of hand between us. I just…"

"Just what?" he asked, a pulse beginning to beat at the base of his skull. Good God, he'd been prepared to cast aside his every belief, his predilection for the fairer sex. Devil take it, he'd decided to change his entire lifestyle for the sake of a woman he'd thought was a man.

Her actually being a woman ought to relieve him. The possibility that this might have been the reason behind the attraction should be a welcome realization. It ought to make him feel better. Except it did not.

Because the point was, he'd been had in the worst way possible.

"I liked you too much to stay away," Harriet whispered. "I'm so sorry."

"Like hell you are," he snarled.

"Please listen. I can explain."

"Nothing you say will ever be good enough.

Harry, the man I was prepared to give up everything for, doesn't exist. He's an illusion."

"We're the same person," she said as tears rolled down her flushed cheeks.

He steeled himself against them – forced himself to be strong. It was likely another trick, intended to manipulate him into showing remorse. He shook his head. "No. You're not. My God… I spoke to you of French letters and how to avoid the pox."

Harriet had, in point of fact, forced him to act dishonorably in every conceivable way.

"I did it for Lucy. Please, Brody, if—"

"I'm either Your Grace or Mr. Evans to you from now on," he informed her darkly. "And you are a charlatan, not a friend. Be warned, I shall never forgive you for this."

"But I—"

Without waiting to hear her out, he stalked from the room, slamming the door behind him. He'd never been so insanely furious in his life. She'd wrecked everything from the very beginning, pretending to be the charming, sweet lad he'd eventually lost his heart to. A heart that was currently shattered into a thousand pieces.

So Harriet Michaels could go and rot for all he cared. He was personally done with her forever.

CHAPTER SEVENTEEN

Harriet scampered out of the bath and snatched up the towel she'd left on a nearby chair. Once dry, she grabbed some padding to stop her courses, put on her trousers, and flung her shirt over her head before bolting from the room. She had to find him. She had to explain.

Barefooted, she ran to the room she suspected was his and proceeded to knock. No answer. She knocked again, then tried the handle. The door opened and she glanced inside the large space which was dwarfed by a massive canopy bed. Blast it, he wasn't there. She shut the door and hastened toward the stairs.

This was precisely what she'd feared, only so much worse because they'd kissed. Had that been just a little over an hour ago? It was hard to imagine with everything turned upside down. Gone was the fondness with which Brody watched her, the heat in his eyes as he'd captured her mouth. In its place had been pure anger and hatred. He loathed her for the deception and who could blame him?

It had been wrong. She should have revealed herself before he discovered the truth. But when, and how, and at what potential cost? Until tonight she'd not believed she could trust him, and by then she'd realized it was too late. As soon as they'd kissed – the moment he'd let down his guard – she'd known confessing the truth could only lead to disaster.

And so it had, without her saying a thing.

Leaping off the second to last step, she landed in the foyer and dashed toward the parlor. This room, too, was empty. Perhaps he'd returned to the library? Not finding him there either and having checked the dining room for good measure, she approached the last remaining door. The one that led to his study.

Shaking from head to toe as a sudden chill gripped her, she struggled to catch her breath before giving the door a few raps. When no one answered, she eased it open and was instantly met by a furious scowl.

"I don't have time for this now," Brody said. Sitting behind his desk, he held a sheet of paper between his hands. "Go to bed. We'll address your deviousness in the morning."

She did her best to brush off his words and failed.

The accusation, so harshly spoken, stung. Her eyes began to prick once again with a fresh onslaught of tears. Speaking without dissolving into a sniveling mess would be hard, but she had to try.

"I only want to explain why I did it." When he said nothing, appearing instead to fight for some sense of calm, she stepped into the room and closed the door. It did not escape her notice that he remained seated, or that he refrained from inviting her to sit. Wringing her hands, she faced him – the man she loved beyond all else – and prayed she'd find the right words. "My sister and I are gentry."

He snorted. "Another thing you lied about. How predictable."

She took a deep breath and willed her heart into a steadier rhythm. Somehow, she'd get through this. "Not a lie, just something I never mentioned."

"A deception nonetheless."

"When Papa died," she said, choosing not to quibble, "the property he owned went to my cousin. When he arrived a week after the funeral, my sister and I were promptly evicted from our childhood home. Papa hadn't thought he'd die young. There wasn't a will, so everything went to the next male heir. Unfortunately he had no interest in taking on the responsibility for two girls. He had his own family, you see, all now happily installed in the house I was born in."

"Sounds like your cousin's a coldhearted bastard,"

Brody said, his voice tight. "But that's no excuse for your behavior."

"Despite being a young lady readying for her debut who lacked any knowledge of hard work, I had no choice but to seek employment," Harriet went on, ignoring his comment for now. "Seeking a position back home where the townsfolk knew me was too humiliating. It also posed the risk of chance encounters with my cousin, which was something I couldn't bear. Besides, I was of the opinion that there was more opportunity in London. Both for myself and Lucy.

"It's also more expensive. Most of the money I'd managed to bring went to finding somewhere to live. This meant securing a job as fast as I could. Thankfully, I managed to find a position at a small florist, immediately off of Bond Street. The wages weren't the best, but the woman who'd employed me was kind. I was happy there, until a gentleman customer took a liking to me and followed me home."

Hands planted on his desk, Brody raised himself out of his chair and leaned forward, his strong arms bracing his body. "This had better end with you kicking him in the ballocks."

"That's exactly what I did."

Brody lowered himself to his chair with a sigh, but kept his frown.

She continued, "I'd never before realized how

vulnerable I was, having always had my father's protection. When I started seeking a new position, I also found there were more positions available, many with much better wages, if I were a man."

"What about a lady's companion or governess? They earn good wages."

"I was sixteen years old, without any London connections. The option wasn't there. I asked, but I was too young and inexperienced. So with all of this taken into account, I decided to crop my hair and dress the part of a working-class boy. The disguise, if convincing, would keep me safe from scoundrels while helping me find better work.

"It wasn't the big success I'd hoped it would be to begin with. I worked as a newsie, a chimney sweep, and a messenger before finally landing the delivery boy job at Hudson & Co. Luckily, Mr. Hudson took a liking to me right away and gave me a chance to do better."

"That still doesn't explain…" He muttered something beneath his breath and bent his head. When he looked back up, his gaze was fierce. "You managed to do the unthinkable, Harriet. And you did so without a second thought."

She shook her head. "You're wrong about that. I did what I could to push you away, turning you down for a drink until I was forced to accept. After that, I tried to keep you at a distance, avoiding you to the best of my ability, but it was no use. You showed up at my door."

"Because I cared for you and for your wellbeing."

"I know."

"You should have refused when I issued the invite for you to stay here. I mean, you must have known what might happen."

"You're right. But the thing of it is I was prepared to risk your anger and the loss of your friendship in order to put Lucy first." Tears ran down her cheeks as she spoke, her voice raw. "She is my sister, my responsibility. It is my duty to do all I can to keep her safe and protect her from harm."

He stared at her hard. "I'll accept that. What I will not accept is you kissing me back."

She had to agree. That had been a very severe lapse in judgement. "I've no excuse for it."

Somehow, disappointment weakened his posture. He crossed his arms and nodded. "Then there's nothing else left to say, is there?"

On the contrary, there was too much. So much she could not get her thoughts in order. Everything was a jumbled mess, her life included. She wished with all her heart she could go and comfort the man she'd wounded. Instead she said, "All I know is that I had to do it. Pushing you away wasn't an option any more. I wanted you too much, even if it would only be for a moment."

He stared at her, his expression annoyingly

inscrutable. "So what was your plan? To tell me tomorrow you'd made a mistake and that it would be best for us just to be friends?"

"Something like that," she admitted, feeling like a despicable cad all over again.

"In doing so, you would have wounded me all the same."

"Perhaps, though not as much as I have now, I wager."

He raked both hands through his hair before rising. Crossing to the sideboard, he poured himself a drink without offering her one, and downed the contents. When he turned to her, his gaze was once again hard as flint. "You have no faith in me, do you?"

Startled by the unexpected question, she instinctively stiffened. "What?"

"It must have occurred to you that I felt a bit more than a passing attraction when I arrived at your lodgings this morning."

"I suppose so," she admitted.

"And yet, when I invited you to come and stay at my home, you didn't think to reveal your secret to me even after I told you my reason for working at Hudson & Co?" When Harriet didn't respond he said, "Do you honestly think I'd have been angrier then, than I am right now? Do you believe I'd have taken back the offer of helping your sister? Are you convinced I'd have gone to Mr.

Hudson and snitched on you? Is that your high opinion of me?"

She couldn't speak. He'd voiced every one of her fears. They'd seemed so reasonable before. Now they felt ridiculous. "I'm so sorry."

"As am I, Harriet." He gave her his back. "You made me question the man I believed myself to be. More than that, you caused me to think I'd be risking my life in order to be with the person you pretended to be. The emotional crisis that's tormented me this past week is incomparable. Do you have any idea how many times I wished for you to be a woman?"

"Wait." She couldn't believe what he was saying. It made her feel like the world was once again tilting. "Are you saying you don't have a preference for men?"

He clenched his jaw while glaring at her. "Exactly so. You are the first. Until we met, I'd only been attracted to women."

Harriet's blood froze in her veins. No wonder he was so furious with her. Good lord. He'd been ready to make an exception for Harry.

"Not that it matters," Brody said. His anger seemed to subside a little, giving way to what looked like regret. "You clearly don't trust me and I sure as hell don't trust you. Without that, what chance do we actually have?"

None.

It felt like her heart had been cleaved in two. What a fool she'd been. This entire debacle was of her own making. She'd caused the pain they both felt in this moment. She and she alone. There was no one else to blame.

Inhaling sharply, she took a step back, retreating on shaky legs. She'd said what she'd come to say and it made little difference. Their relationship was still ruined. He wouldn't forgive her.

Swallowing hard, she reached for the door, blindly fumbling for the handle while making up her mind to leave in the morning. Unfortunately, Lucy would have to suffer the consequence of her actions as well. She sniffed on that thought as regret tore her to bits.

Her hand connected with the doorknob. She stumbled a step and then squeaked when the door was pushed open, straight into her spine.

"What on... Dear me, I'm terribly sorry. Didn't think anyone would be standing right there." The words came from a gentleman who appeared to be more or less her own age. He grabbed her elbow, steadying her.

Brody sighed. "You're punctual for a change."

The other man shrugged. "I figured the situation might warrant a bit more gravitas than usual."

"Since you're here, I suppose introductions are in order," Brody murmured. He frowned at Harriet, his scrutinous gaze making her very aware of her state of undress. "Finley, allow me to present Miss Harriet Michaels. Harriet, this is my brother, the Marquess of Losturn."

"A pleasure," Harriet said, crossing her arms, then uncrossing them again.

"Likewise." Losturn smirked. An uncomfortable degree of interest lit up his eyes. He glanced at his brother. "I wasn't aware you'd acquired a new mistress."

"I haven't." Brody clipped the words.

"Just a one-night tumble then?" Losturn gave a thoughtful nod. "Makes sense, considering the finances and all that."

"Finn…" Brody warned, his voice hard.

"You've clearly acquired a taste for something different, Brother." Losturn grinned. "Are the men's clothes and short hair a newly acquired fetish of yours?"

Harriet leapt back, barely managing to avoid getting trampled as Brody lunged for his brother. He grabbed him by the throat and shoved him against the wall.

CHAPTER EIGHTEEN

A painting clattered to the floor. Finn wheezed. His hands gripped Brody's arms and hands in an effort to make him loosen his hold.

"Take it back," Brody hissed. He pulled his brother away from the wall and slammed him against it once more. They'd not fought like this since they were children, scuffling about in the dirt. "You'll not disrespect my guest."

Finn pushed back, causing Brody to lose his balance. He tripped in an effort to regain his footing and fell to the floor, taking his brother down with him.

"Brody," Finn gasped as he managed to get free and started to scramble away. "You're mad."

Brody caught him by the ankle and yanked him backward. His head connected with the floor.

"Augh!"

"You will apologize to me," Brody snarled, forcing himself up and pinning Finn down. "And to Miss Michaels. This instant. Or so help me, you'll not be attending that duel. I'll bloody well kill you myself."

"Jesus, Brody." Finn twisted and tried to shove Brody away. "She must be a really good shag to have you so—"

Brody's fist connected with Finn's jaw. "You're speaking of a gentlewoman, not a whore."

Finn stared up at Brody. "But…I could see her nipples through that—"

Brody punched him again. "You'll forget about that if you've got any sense. Now, are you going to apologize or do I need to keep hitting you?"

Finn brought his hands up to shield his face. "No. I mean yes. I'll apologize, Brody. Of course I will. I'm sorry."

Huffing a breath, Brody stood and reached for his brother's hand so he could haul him to his feet. He straightened his jacket and turned to find the space behind him empty.

"Where did she go?" Finn asked, giving voice to Brody's thoughts.

"She must have left when we tumbled to the floor." He sent his brother a sidelong glance and saw that a bruise was rapidly forming on his right cheek. "Do you want a slab of meat to dull the pain?"

Finn shook his head, then headed for the sideboard where he poured himself a large glass of brandy. "I can't believe you actually punched me."

"I'll do it again if you don't watch that reckless tongue of yours."

"I'm almost afraid to ask," Finn said, "but would you have come to blows with me if I'd insulted someone else? Or is Miss Michaels of particular interest?"

Brody sighed and went to return the fallen painting to the wall. "It's complicated."

"I'm the king of complicated, Brody." Finn grinned and gulped down some brandy. "So tell me about it."

"I'd rather not."

"Why?"

For a thousand different reasons.

"Because it's personal, that's why."

Finn tracked Brody as he walked to his chair and waited until he was seated before stating, "You're in love with her."

Brody raised an eyebrow. "Watch it."

Finn scoffed. He dropped into one of the two chairs that stood across from the desk, spilling some of his drink. "Deny it as much as you like, but you've never been this protective of any woman before. Admit it."

His brother was right. The elemental need to come to Harriet's defense had been instant and fierce. It went beyond the protectiveness Finn spoke of.

"Fine. I'll allow that I might be slightly smitten." He was also very upset and hurt, not to mention unsure of what to do next where she was concerned. Initially, he'd been compelled to lash out and push her away. He'd wanted to distance himself from her as much as possible. He scrubbed his jaw and considered Finn who was wearing the most annoying smirk he'd ever seen. "She tricked me though. Turns out she's not who she claimed to be."

Finn's expression turned serious. He appeared to mull that statement over for a moment before asking, "Was there ill-intent behind her deception?"

"No."

"Then what's the problem?"

"What's the problem?" Brody gaped at his brother. "The person I fell for doesn't exist, Finn. I lost my heart to a damn lie."

"Are you sure about that?" When Brody didn't respond right away Finn pressed, "Papa always said love is born from the harmony found between two well-matched souls. It's not external, so it should have nothing to do with who Miss Michaels may have claimed to be, but rather with who she is right here." He pressed his fist to his chest. "Focus on that and I'm sure you'll find the connection you shared is real."

Brody sank against his chair in baffled silence.

Not in a million years would he have expected his scamp of a brother to impart such words of wisdom.

Swallowing, he acknowledged the tightness in his chest and the way his pulse fluttered with newfound hope. The clock on a nearby shelf ticked as he pondered the threat he'd made Harriet earlier – of severing ties with her forever.

A sharp pain pierced his heart, causing him to wince as he realized that losing her would likely kill him. Because…

The truth of it was that she and Harry were one and the same. If anything, Harriet was all the more impressive because of the sacrifice she had made in order to care for her sister. By choosing to live as a man, she'd given up her identity as a woman, denying herself the chance to meet a man who might love her for who she truly was.

She was kind, caring, and utterly selfless while he… He was beginning to think he might be a bit of a moron. Because the more he sat there, allowing Finn's words to settle more fully inside his thick head, he realized it wasn't Harry he loved. It was Harriet. It had been all along. Without her, Harry could not have existed.

He stared at his brother. "That is shockingly insightful of you."

"I have my moments." Finn grinned.

"Apparently so." Brody glanced at his desk where Finn's will awaited. The hour was getting late. They ought to start with the necessary adjustments. He'd have to put the matter pertaining to Harriet Michaels on hold for the moment. With this in mind he told Finn, "The duel is in six hours. If we're to get some sleep before then, I suggest we proceed."

"Agreed."

Finn reached for the papers and started reviewing, yet despite his best efforts, Brody could not get Harriet out of his mind. She was stuck there. During their acquaintance, she had become the person he looked forward to seeing most every morning.

She was more than kind, caring, and selfless. And he couldn't imagine his life without her.

This notion stayed with him as he retired a half hour later. It made it impossible for him to sleep. The need to speak with her – to try and resolve their differences – kept him from rest. Which meant that he was awake and able to hear the rush of footsteps in the hallway at two in the morning.

Curious to know what was going on, he shoved the blankets aside and climbed from his bed. After getting dressed quickly, he left his room and paused to listen. A faint groan caught his attention, and he instantly worried Lucy had taken a turn for the worse.

Intent on checking to see if the doctor might have been sent for, he hurried in the direction from which the sound had come. But when he poked his head inside Lucy's room, all was quiet. He closed the door gently and tilted his head. It sounded like someone was bustling about in the room next door where Harriet slept. Brody approached, stilling when he heard an agonized whimper. The muffled voice of a woman followed.

Determined to know what was going on, Brody gave the door a quick knock and nudged it open just enough to peer inside. What he saw nearly stopped his heart.

The vibrant person who'd muddled his mind beyond reason had been reduced to a sickly individual. Harriet's face was pale and tears swam in her eyes. Wrapped in a simple dressing gown fashioned from coarse white linen, she clutched at her stomach.

"Looks like he's got the same ailment his sister's been suffering from," said Betsy, the elderly maid who'd come to Harriet's aid. "I've only just managed to um…get him back into bed. He was sitting on the floor when I arrived, over by the bell-pull."

The words were barely spoken before Harriet retched and vomited into a vase. The flowers that had previously filled said vase were scattered across the carpet.

"Go away," Harriet groaned. "I… Oh no…"

Brody's chest tightened. Without thinking he rushed forward, perching himself on the edge of the bed and stroking her back while she vomited once again.

"I've got you," he soothed before glancing at the maid. "A bucket, if you will, and maybe a cup of hot tea along with some water. I'll stay with Mr. Michaels while you fetch it."

"Of course, Your Grace." The maid left.

"Would you like me to send for the doctor?" Brody asked. He took the vase from Harriet's hands and set it aside on the floor. She shook her head without meeting his gaze. Reaching up, he brushed a strand of hair from her cheek and tucked it behind her ear. "Something else perhaps?"

"No."

"You'll be all right in a couple of days. Lucy's already faring better and you clearly have the same thing." It was imperative he be as optimistic as possible even though his gut was twisted into a tight knot. It felt like his chest had been chopped open by a blunt axe. Seeing her in pain and feeling like he could do nothing but wait for her to recover was awful.

She closed her eyes and took a deep breath, then slowly released it while lying back. A tear appeared at the corner of one eye before trickling down her cheek. Brody swept it aside with his finger.

"Please go away," she muttered.

"I'm afraid I can't do that."

She swallowed and turned her head so she stared not at him but at the wall when next she spoke. "Why not?"

"Because..." He grabbed her hand and gave it a squeeze. "Despite everything, there's no denying I care for you as a person, whether that person be Harry or Harriet."

She pressed her lips together, her entire body beginning to tremble as she started weeping in earnest. "You don't have to treat me well just because I'm sick."

"Harriet, I—"

She wrenched her hand free from his and turned onto her side, offering him her back. "You were right. Everything you said is true. I'm a horrible person for what I did. Our kiss should never have happened. I should have been honest with you and perhaps then... I don't know. I'm so incredibly sorry."

"As am I," Brody whispered. "I was shocked and confused when I realized you were a woman. And then I got so bloody angry. Not because you'd fooled me, but because you'd convinced me to turn my back on who I've always been. You made me want to reach for a different kind of future with Harry."

"Only Harry doesn't exist." She took a ragged breath while Brody set his hand gently upon her shoulder.

"But Harriet does." He moved his thumb back and forth with soothing strokes and prepared to say something more, but then the maid returned and he lost the chance.

Brody took the tray she brought and set it on the bedside table. The vase was whisked away, and a bucket placed next to the bed. Brody glanced at the clock. It was nearing three.

"The tea is here, if you'd like some," he told Harriet. When she didn't answer, he moved to the other side of the bed and crouched in front of her face. Her eyes were closed, her lips slightly parted in slumber. He set his palm carefully to her forehead and frowned in response to the heat he felt there.

Straightening, he turned to Betsy. "I believe he's got a fever. Can you please stay with him for a bit while I go wake my brother? He's got an early meeting he can't afford to miss."

"Of course, Your Grace. I'm happy to watch over Mr. Michaels for as long as you need."

"Thank you. I'll make certain you have time for a nap later."

The maid nodded and Brody went to get Finn out of bed. With the duel scheduled for five, they'd have to depart within the hour in order to make it to Hackney Meadow on time. Having reached Finn's bedchamber door, Brody knocked.

"Come!"

Brody entered the room which was fully lit by two oil lamps. Already dressed, Finn was in the process of tying his cravat. His gaze swept over Brody.

"You're not fully dressed."

"I thought it best to make sure you were up first."

"As you can see, I'm almost ready."

"Did you sleep?"

"I couldn't. Doesn't look like you were able to either."

"Too many thoughts." Finn nodded and Brody took a moment to consider his overall appearance. "The ruby-tipped cravat pin suits you best. You should wear it."

"Thank you." Finn collected the pin from a box that stood on top of his dresser and pushed it through his cravat. "How's that?"

Brody approached and paused when he was a foot away from his brother. Reaching up, he adjusted the pin. "Perfect."

"I'll go grab some biscuits from the kitchen. We can eat them on the way."

"Betsy brought Miss Michaels some tea a short while ago, so there might be hot water left on the kettle. If so, I'd appreciate a cup of coffee before we go. Do you think you can manage that?"

Finn snorted. "What do you take me for? A help-less toff?"

"I wouldn't dare," Brody told him gravely. Their father had always insisted they knew how to tend to their basic needs. He'd insisted Cook teach them both how to use a range to boil water and fry simple food. Their father had been a wise man indeed and Brody missed him dearly. The ache in his chest when he thought of him hadn't diminished much since his death. It still had the weight of a thousand anvils bearing down on his chest.

Finn left for the kitchen while Brody returned to his room. He'd wanted to check on Harriet on the way, but dared not waste the time. So he got dressed quickly and checked the clock. He still had half an hour to spare.

Returning to Harriet's room, he glanced at Betsy. "Can you please check on Lucy?"

Betsy bobbed a quick curtsey and went to do her master's bidding, allowing Brody a moment of privacy with the woman who'd turned his entire world upside down. Her slumber was peaceful, he noted. She'd likely sleep like this for a while, oblivious to his stepping out to serve as Finn's second.

If only he didn't have to go. If only he could remain here at Harriet's side. He approached the bed and checked her temperature with his palm, stilling as each of his heartbeats slowed in response. She felt hotter than she had fifteen minutes before. Unease swept his spine. Lucy had not been quite this hot. Had she?

Determined to do what he could, he grabbed the washcloth that hung by the washstand and dipped it in water. Once he'd wrung it, he crossed to the bed, nudged at Harriet until she shifted onto her back, and placed the damp cloth on her brow. She groaned and became slightly restless before settling back into deep sleep.

"Lucy appears to be well," said Betsy. "She's sleeping peacefully."

So was Harriet. "Did you check her forehead?"

"Yes, Your Grace. She's cool to the touch. I believe she's on the mend."

As relieved as Brody was to hear this, his heart still hurt over having to leave Harriet's side. In one short fortnight she'd become everything to him. He couldn't stand the idea of being parted from her while she suffered, of not knowing whether she was improving or…

No. He could not think like that. It was just a stomach upset brought on by something she'd eaten. She'd recover, all would be well, and he'd…

Brody stared at her sleeping form.

In his anger, he'd said things that couldn't be unsaid. He'd deliberately lashed out with every intention of wounding, and he was fairly certain he'd succeeded. What difference did it make if she'd wronged him? Right now, his greatest concern was whether or not they could find a way past all of this. Did she even care for him as deeply as he cared for her?

"Brody?" He turned at the sound of his brother's voice and blinked. "What are you doing in here?"

"She's sick, Finn." God, he could barely speak, his throat was so hoarse.

"With the same thing Lucy's got?"

"I think so."

Finn glanced at the bed. "When did you find out?"

"Right before coming to wake you." He swept one hand across his brow and hung his head while attempting to work up the strength required to leave this room. "Her fever seems to be rising."

When Finn said nothing, Brody tightened his muscles and forced his body to straighten. He could not – would not – fall apart on account of this. He'd faced worse. This would pass. He turned to the door with decisive movements. "We need to get going."

"*I* need to get going," Finn said. "You've got to stay here."

"Impossible. You need me there as your second."

"I'll wake Rhys and ask him to come in your stead."

"No." Brody shook his head. "You're about to engage in a duel, Finn. What sort of brother would I be if I weren't there to support you?"

Finn placed one hand on Brody's shoulder and met his gaze. "The sort who attempted to stop me from ending up in this situation to begin with. I should have listened."

"Finn, I—"

"She needs you too, Brody. More, I'll wager, considering she's feeling wretched in a strange house. It would be good for her to find you here when she wakes. Besides, what brother would *I* be if I made you choose me over the woman you love?"

"It's my duty to be there for you when you need me, Finn. I have to protect you."

"Not anymore." Finn, moved to the door. "She's your future now, Brody. I'll fetch Rhys and then I'll be off. I'll see you later."

"Don't get yourself killed," Brody warned.

Finn waved him off as he disappeared into the hallway. "It's only to first blood. I'll be fine."

Brody dearly hoped so. He was still considering hurrying after him when the front door slammed shut ten minutes later. After crossing to the window, he glanced down at the street below where Finn proceeded to flag down a hackney.

Poor Rhys, who'd been dragged from his bed one hour too early with no time to dress, was still buttoning his jacket before climbing into the carriage Finn had acquired. The conveyance set off and Brody's shoulders slumped in response to the guilt that now gripped him.

He should have gone with his brother. It was wrong of him not to.

A soft murmur rose from behind him. Turning, he saw that Harriet squirmed beneath the covers. He rushed to her side and felt the washcloth he'd draped across her brow. It was warm to the touch and would have to be soaked in cool water once more.

But when he prepared to see to the task, Harriet

produced such an agonized groan, it froze him in place. He stared at her, unsure of what he should do as her breaths quickened and she moved her head side to side. "I need…"

Snapping out of his trance at the realization she faced the wrong way, Brody rushed to collect the bucket. He barely managed to get it under her head before it was too late. Convulsive movements shook her as her stomach attempted to rid itself of additional contents, but there was hardly anything left.

"I think you should drink something," he said once she'd settled against her pillows once more. He collected the washcloth, which had fallen into her lap, and used it to wipe her mouth. "It will make it easier on your muscles if there's something for you to cast up."

"No," she said in a barely-there whisper. She gave her head a violent shake.

Deciding she'd probably be all right for the next few minutes, Brody decided to let the matter rest as he went to rinse the washcloth. Selecting a clean one, he soaked it, wrung it, and placed it on her brow.

She sighed as though with welcome relief. "Thank you."

"You're welcome." He considered the untouched teacup that sat on the bedside table and decided to fill it. Once this was done, he swept one arm under Harriet's back.

"What are you doing?"

"Helping you sit so you can drink."

"I said no."

"Don't be so bloody stubborn and let me care for you, will you?"

She tried to twist away. "Have you forgotten how much you hate me?"

He stilled before lowering into a crouch and pulling her into his arms so he could embrace her. "I could never hate you, Harriet. Not in a million years."

"How is that possible?"

"We'll discuss it once you're better. For now, I'd suggest some tea."

She sent the teacup a hesitant look as she withdrew from Brody's arms. "I don't think I can."

"Please try."

Moving slowly, with hesitant movements, she set the cup to her lips and drank. When she returned the cup to the bedside table, Brody was glad to see it was more than half empty.

"Well done." He stood and tucked the blankets around her. "How do you feel?"

She eyed him with an are-you-seriously-asking-me-that kind of look. "Awful. As though the slightest movement will see that tea end up in the bucket."

"Maybe I should send for the doctor." He glanced at the floor. "Have you made use of the chamber pot too?"

"What do you think?" she asked, her tone grumpy.

He nodded. "I'll have one of the maids come and fetch it."

"I'd rather see to it myself."

"You're in no position to do so and well you know it." When her only response to this was a sullen look, he said, "It's a good thing you managed to put on that dressing gown prior to Betsy's arrival. As far as I know, she still believes you to be Mr. Michaels instead of Miss Michaels."

"Sorry. My head hurts…Your Grace. I can't follow your logic."

"I know what I said when we argued, but can we please go back to being informal?" When she gave a small nod he told her, "The shirt you wore when you came to my study last night was more revealing than you probably realized. Anyone who saw you like that would have known you're a woman. It was…obvious."

Harriet stared at him a moment and then her lips parted on a small gasp as she squeezed her eyes shut. "Just when I though it couldn't get worse."

"Do you think you can keep up the act?"

"Of course. I've been living as Harry for over two years."

"Good. Because having an unmarried gentle-woman staying beneath the same roof as two bache-lors would make for quite the scandal."

"I…" She tuned on her side and proceeded to cast up her tea.

Brody swallowed a curse and sat down beside her, doing whatever he could to add a small bit of comfort.

CHAPTER NINETEEN

Harriet couldn't recall being so sick before, and that included her wretched bouts of influenza and chickenpox when she was younger. Her stomach burned while feeling as though it were being cut open by shards of glass. And the nausea. It was relentless. She knew only a few moments of peace immediately after being sick before it descended upon her again.

She felt worse than wretched. As luck would have it, Brody – the man whose high opinion she craved – was here to witness it all. If only he'd vanish. But no. He remained, despite her insistence he leave.

Closing her eyes, she forced back the tears that threatened once more. She'd betrayed his trust. She'd taken advantage of his desire for Harry, and in so doing she'd stolen something that never should have been hers.

She had lied in the most spectacular way imaginable. Brody was only setting his anger aside out of pity.

What about him though? Is he who you thought him to be?

No. He was a duke of all things. But at least he'd not pretended to be a member of the opposite sex. She closed her eyes to block him from view, even as he removed the compress from her brow and replaced it with a fresh one.

"You're burning up," he murmured. "I think it's time for more drastic measures."

Whatever that might entail, Harriet was fairly certain it would involve her wanting to die. She had to distract him somehow. "When's the last time anyone checked on Lucy?"

"Betsy did so around three. Lucy was sound asleep at the time and showed no sign of fever." The heels of his shoes scraped the floor. She could sense him moving toward the part of the room where the bell pull hung. "I'm going to send a footman to fetch the doctor, and then you're getting back in the tub. It hasn't been emptied."

"What?" She hugged the blankets around her and tried to scoot farther underneath them in an attempt to hide. Lord, it felt as though her eyes were on fire.

"The water will have cooled hours ago. It should

help reduce your fever better than these useless compresses."

"I'm not getting back in the tub," she muttered from under her blankets. "Definitely not while you're here."

"You most certainly are," he said in an authoritarian tone she'd not heard him use before. "If it makes you more comfortable, you may get in fully clothed. I care not as long as it helps cool you down."

"If anyone needs cooling down, it is you," Harriet muttered.

"What was that?"

She groaned as a sudden sharp pain speared her stomach. When would this hellish nightmare end? Hissing a breath, she listened to Brody moving about. If he thought he'd wrestle her into the tub, he was sorely mistaken. She'd resist, despite her weakened state.

"You called, Your Grace?" a woman's voice asked.

"Please have either Jimmy or William fetch Doctor Heartfelt. They may tell him the matter pertains to a feverish houseguest."

"I'll see to it straight away," said the woman.

A rustling sound, followed by the fading tap-tap of footsteps, alerted Harriet to the maid's departure. "That's not the doctor who tended to Lucy."

"It's the man my family's been using since I was a child," Brody said. "I thought a second opinion might be useful."

Maybe, though Harriet doubted it. She was fairly certain she just had to suffer the course of whatever this was.

"He doesn't live too far from here, so I reckon he'll arrive within the hour. That gives us enough time for a quick dip."

Harriet clutched at her blanket. "I already…told you. I'm…not…getting…into…"

Things truly weren't going too well when she lacked the energy to speak. She slumped beneath the weight of the very air filling the room. Her body burned, her eyes stung, and it felt like nails were being driven into her skull.

"Easy does it," Brody murmured while pushing her into a sitting position. "We'll just remove this."

"Don't have to," she groaned, her words slurring.

"You'll be glad it's not wet when you get back out."

Too weak to protest any further, she leaned against him while he went to work on removing her robe. It slid from around her, leaving her in nothing more than her nightgown.

Strong arms slid beneath her and scooped her up into the air. Her head fell against a firm chest, beneath which she could feel the steady beat of Brody's heart. She clutched at his shirt and held on tight as he crossed the room with her.

When he lowered her into the water a few seconds later, she'd expected to gasp in response to the chill. Instead, she found it a welcome relief from the heat that consumed her. Which could only mean that she really had been in need of cooling down and that he'd been correct to act as he did.

It was thoughtful of him to do so. In fact, his every action so far was proof that he cared for her deeply. Perhaps as deeply as she cared for him? Was such a thing possible after what she'd put him through? He had said he didn't hate her. After tonight she was inclined to believe him.

But where did that leave them?

He was still a duke and she was still a nobody doing her best to make ends meet. They were completely mismatched.

"Feel a bit better?" he asked. He'd dropped to a crouch beside the tub so his face was level with hers.

"Yes." It was all she could manage to say.

His hand found her cheek and she pressed herself to it, enjoying the calming effect of his touch. It wouldn't last. She'd recover and leave his home, return to her own dismal lodgings and get on with life. As would he. Not out of choice perhaps, but out of necessity. He'd realize soon enough that even if he could forgive her for what she'd done, and even if he was still interested in a future with her, it could never be.

Men like him didn't marry women like her. And she would never be any man's mistress. Not even his.

Which only made her feel worse when he pressed

his lips to her brow. No words were uttered, but the gesture spoke volumes. It conveyed the contents of his heart, shattering hers in the process.

So she wept as he helped her from the tub shortly after. Not so much because of the fever this time, but because of the loss she was already mourning. Oh, how she wished she might have had a Season and come to London as planned. Perhaps she could have met Brody in a ballroom then. Although he would still have been miles above her in social status, at least she'd have had a chance.

"We need to get you into dry clothes." He was already sweeping her nightgown up over her head while she stood like a statue, no longer caring if he saw her naked. All she wanted was comfort, her inhibitions be damned. "This will have to go too. Do you have others you can use?"

She blinked. "What?"

"The padding for your courses," he said, drying her with brisk movements. "I'm sorry, but I didn't realize until now. The water soaked the one you are wearing, so you'll need to change it before returning to bed."

Of course.

To her absolute shock and dismay, she wasn't the least bit embarrassed about him seeing her like this. She was at her worst, stripped of clothing, with her vomit filling a bucket just a few paces away, and blood about to stain the sheets unless he helped her stop it. Ordinarily, she probably would have leapt from the nearest window in shame, but she was beyond caring about the pathetic state she was in.

The only thing on her mind was returning to bed and getting more rest.

"Check my bag. The padding should be at the bottom."

He wrapped the towel tightly around her and went to search through her things. She watched in stupefied silence. The situation was so incredibly strange it almost felt like a dream.

"Here we are." He held up one hand and glanced at her over his shoulder. "What do you use to hold it in place?"

"There should be some long lengths of linen."

He rummaged around some more and finally stood, a victorious look on his face as he showed her the items he'd found. And then he suddenly laughed while shaking his head. "Sorry, but this is by far the oddest situation I've ever found myself in."

She managed a tiny grin despite feeling slightly dizzy. "I was…thinking…the same."

All traces of humor vanished from his expression, and he was suddenly there, steadying her before she lost her balance. "Let's finish up so you can lie down. Don't overthink it, just let me help."

It took her a second to grasp his meaning, but as soon as she did she almost bolted, jerking to one side so quickly she nearly tumbled back into the tub.

Leaning back, she stuck out her palm to keep him at a safe distance. "I…I can manage. Thank you."

He gave her a skeptical look though his shoulders did droop with what looked like relief. Nevertheless, he told her gently, "It's nothing to fuss about. Least of all in the state you're in."

Was he mad?

"I am not letting you help me with this," she gritted, forcing all of her strength into each word. "Just…leave the padding and bindings there, on that stool, and I…I'll take care of it."

He did not look convinced. "You can barely keep yourself upright."

"Brody." She took a ragged breath and grabbed the edge of the tub when she felt herself sway to one side. "Please go."

Instead of budging, he crossed his arms. "I'd rather not leave you alone, but I promise upon my honor that I will refrain from looking while you tend to yourself. Will that do?"

Too weak to argue any further, she agreed and waited until he'd presented her with his back before ridding herself of the soaked padding. Moving slowly while leaning her weight against the tub, she put fresh ones in their place then wrapped the towel around herself once more.

"I'm…ready," she said, hugging her trembling body.

Leaping back into motion, Brody retrieved a dry

shirt and dropped it over her head, then pulled her arms through the sleeves.

"There." Standing before her, he ran his hands up and down her arms with long soothing strokes. "That should do it."

"Thank you."

The desire she'd seen in his eyes when they'd stood in his library yesterday evening had been replaced by tender concern. His hands assessed her cheeks and her brow while searching her face with his gaze. She watched as his throat worked, straining as he swallowed.

"You're still very warm." The whispered words fluttered across her nose. "Come. Let's get you to bed and we'll see about cleaning your teeth."

She rolled her eyes but allowed him to do as he wished. If he ever needed to seek additional work, she had no doubt he'd do well as a lady's maid.

"How's your stomach faring?" he asked once he'd gathered supplies. "Any nausea right now?"

She took a deep breath and expelled it slowly to test the state she was in. Her stomach seemed to have settled. "No."

"Let me know if that changes. I'd hate to make you feel worse." He glanced at the clock on her dresser, studying it as if with concern.

"What is it?" she asked.

He swallowed, then shook his head swiftly and forced a smile. "Nothing."

Without adding anything further, he put some powder on a small silver brush and ran it along her teeth with light scrubbing motions. Holding a small glass bowl he'd collected from next to the wash stand, he urged her to spit, before handing her the rest of her tea.

She drank while he cleaned away the supplies. There was something so temptingly domestic about it. The night they'd just shared was so intimate, she wondered if she would ever know such closeness with anyone else.

When he returned to her bedside, he perched on the edge of the mattress. The smile he gave her was filled with such adoration, she longed to throw her arms around him and hold onto him forever.

"How are you feeling?"

"Hot and uncomfortable."

"And your stomach?"

"I think it may have settled."

"That's excellent news. I'll ask Cook to make you some toast once the doctor has been to see you. I'm sure he'll arrive any moment but..." He tilted his head at the sound of a downstairs door opening and closing. Approaching footsteps sounded.

Brody swooped in and pressed his mouth to hers with possessive force. The kiss took no more than a second, but it certainly left her fevered brain reeling. She gasped and stared at him in wonder as he leapt away from the bed and positioned himself near the washstand. When the footman arrived with the doctor, all the two men saw was a worried host trying to make his guest comfortable by preparing a compress.

"Doctor Heartfelt," Brody said, his voice so calm and serious, it completely clashed with Harriet's riotous state of being. "Thank you for coming at such an early hour. I believe the ailment my guest is suffering from is due to something he ate before he arrived. Nevertheless, I thought it best to check since the fever appears to be high."

The doctor scanned the room for a moment before approaching the bed. Wary of his studious gaze, Harriet drew her blankets all the way up to the tip of her nose. Stopping beside her, the doctor pressed his hand to her forehead. "I agree. Can you please go over the symptoms for me?"

Brody did so while Harriet closed her eyes. They were so hot and tired they hurt.

"It is worth noting," Brody finished, "that Mr. Michaels's sister has suffered a similar illness, from which she is now recovering."

"And how long did her symptoms last?" asked the doctor.

"One day."

"Then it's likely something they ate. Had it been something more severe, it would have persisted much longer."

"Mr. Michaels's symptoms seem pretty severe to me," Brody grumbled.

A pause followed before the doctor suggested, "I can provide a more thorough examination of your guest if you wish, Your Grace, but to do so we'll have to remove the covers and have him sit up."

Propelled by pure dread, Harriet flung her head over the side of the bed and proceeded to retch while spitting into the bucket and groaning.

"Thank you," Brody said, "but I don't believe he's up for that. Besides, I'm sure you've made an accurate diagnosis as usual."

"He should recover as long as he gets enough rest," the doctor added while Harriet kept up her act, which wasn't hard to do, considering the state she was in. "Be sure to give him plenty of fluids to compensate for what he's lost. And feed him as soon as he's able to hold food down. Toast and porridge are my recommendation."

Exactly what the other doctor had said about Lucy.

"And the fever?" Brody asked.

"It would appear that you're managing that as well as possible, judging from the compress you're holding and the fact that it looks like that tub was recently used. I can suggest nothing more, besides having one of your maids tend to him while you rest."

"Thank you."

There was a pause before the doctor said, "If that is all, I fear I must be going."

"I'll see you out," Brody said.

As soon as the room fell quiet, Harriet scrambled from the bed and located the chamber pot. Even though she could barely stand or see, she managed to make quick use of it and was back in bed, tucked under the blankets, before Brody returned. She expelled a long breath. There was only so much lack of dignity she could muster. Despite everything else he'd assisted her with, having him watch her empty her bladder was not to be born.

She slid farther under the blankets and was curled into a tight ball when she heard him walk into the room. "What time is it?"

"Almost four." His voice sounded strained, most likely because of exhaustion.

He ought to get some sleep. So should she. Going to work tomorrow would be… Oh God…she couldn't afford to miss one more day.

"You've got to send word." A chill swept over her shoulders. She shivered, no longer hot but chilled to the bone. Her teeth began chattering. "Mr. Hudson must know…I…can't…work."

"Christ, Harriet." Brody was instantly there, his strong body climbing into the bed behind her. Undoing the blanket with which she'd cocooned herself, he pulled her snug up against his warm frame and blew hot air against the top of her back.

Unable to resist the soothing effect of being held and cared for by him, she snuggled closer. "I hope I don't get you sick."

"I think that's unlikely. I'm fairly certain your ailment is linked to the baked goods you ate. The delay between you and Lucy eating those pies coincides pretty well with the time between each of you developing symptoms. The doctor agrees."

"Yes, but—"

"Would you like me to fetch some toast?"

"I'm too...tired..."

"Rest then. You can eat when you wake."

His lips brush the back of her neck. Harriet sighed and allowed herself to relax against him while drifting off to sleep.

When she woke, sunlight filled the room, but Brody was gone.

CHAPTER TWENTY

Sending a note to Mr. Hudson did not feel sufficient. Considering how well he'd treated Harriet, offering her a promotion she probably wouldn't have gotten elsewhere, Brody decided it would be best to meet him in person. It would also be easier for Brody to convince Mr. Hudson of his need to keep Harriet on, if it came to that.

He set off after eating a quick breakfast and left the servants with instructions to give Mr. Michaels some toast, should he wake before Brody returned. It was almost six-thirty. The duel would have ended a while ago and Finn would soon be returning.

Hopefully in one piece.

Whenever Brody had glanced at a clock last night, he'd thought of Finn and how he was faring. He hastened his strides, praying he'd manage to get home before his brother.

Thankfully, Mr. Hudson, a self-proclaimed morning man, had already opened the office when Brody showed up. He entered the office and approached the man's desk with every intention of seeing to Harriet's best interests.

"Good morning, Mr. Hudson."

"You're earlier than usual today, Mr. Evans. Good to see you. There's some tea in the back room if you'd like to help yourself to a cup before the others get here."

"Thank you, but I fear I'm unable to stay." He pulled up a chair and sat so he could face his employer with greater directness. "I went back to check on Mr. Michaels yesterday – to see if he needed help with his sister."

"That was very good of you." Mr. Hudson studied Brody. "It's unusual for the editors and the print staff to mingle. Most of the men out here in the front consider themselves better than those who've got ink-stained fingers."

"An arrogant point of view," Brody muttered, "and not one I share. If anything, the print staff have the harder work, yet they accomplish it like a well-oiled machine."

"I'm of a like mind. Mr. Michaels alone is more indispensable than anyone else in my employ."

"It's good to hear you say so since it will no doubt make this conversation a great deal simpler. Unfortunately, Mr. Michaels has caught the same thing that brought his sister low. He ought to be ready for work the day after tomorrow, but until then, he needs to rest."

Mr. Hudson's eyebrows dipped in response to his frown. "I cannot afford for him to be absent another day. Not without someone else stepping in."

"I'd do so if I were able, but I can't." Brody would not budge on this. He had to see Finn and beyond that, he'd no intention of leaving Harriet until he knew she was fully recovered.

"I'm sorry, but you must understand. The press is at a virtual standstill until he resumes his work. I've got three men waiting for him to show up. What are they supposed to do in the meantime?"

"Oliver's able to fill the sorts. It won't be as fast without a reader, but some of the work will get done."

Mr. Hudson shook his head. "I'm sorry, but I have to find a proper replacement this instant. Work on the manuscript you recommended needs to commence if we're to get the book into shops before Christmas."

"A day or two won't prevent that from happening," Brody insisted. "Mr. Michaels is a hard worker. More than that, he's the best there is."

"I agree, which is why this decision is so bloody hard to make. But the fact of the matter is, he isn't here."

"Considering the state he's in, I can't imagine

you'd want him here." Brody raked his hair with his fingers. "He's been vomiting all night and has one hell of a fever. He can barely stand, yet you're ready to punish him for remaining in bed."

"As much as I sympathize, it doesn't change the fact that I'm losing money while he's away. He's the most critical part of this enterprise, Mr. Evans. Surely you understand why I'm forced to do what I must to keep my business operational."

"It's just for a day or two," Brody repeated.

"And I wish I could afford to wait, but I can't." He grabbed a piece of paper and started writing TYPE-SETTER NEEDED WITH IMMEDIATE EFFECT.

"He'll be back as soon as he's fully recovered," Brody said as he shoved to his feet. "In case you've not yet found a replacement or the new man doesn't work out. You can decide what to do then."

Mr. Hudson glanced at Brody. "You're an honorable man, looking out for your friend in this way. I'm impressed, so I'll agree to consider taking him back if he does decide to stop by. In the meantime..." He stood and crossed to the window where he proceeded to post the notice. Turning, he shoved his hands in his pockets and met Brody's gaze. "What about you?"

"I already told you I can't stay today."

Mr. Hudson responded with a slow nod before grabbing a second piece of paper on which he announced the need for Brody's replacement. It was fine. Brody didn't need the job. It had just been the means to an end, right?

"Thank you for the chance you gave me," Brody informed Mr. Hudson. He offered his hand and Mr. Hudson shook it. "Good luck with *A Seductive Scandal.*"

"*A Seductive Scandal?*"

"The title I had in mind for the novel."

"A bit risqué," Mr. Hudson murmured while tapping the edge of his mouth with one finger, "but it will certainly draw attention. I'll keep it in mind."

Brody tipped his hat in parting and left with an unhappy sense of unease in his stomach. He regretted having to leave since he'd gotten on well with his colleagues. Staying, however, would be impossible when his conscience compelled him to put his brother and Harriet first. And besides, he didn't actually need the job.

But for Harriet, losing her source of income would be disastrous. Worse was the fact that she viewed her profession as more than the means with which to get by. She genuinely enjoyed her work. Finding out she might not be welcomed back would crush her.

Unhappy, Brody shoved his hands in his pockets and strode away, his posture hunched. The early morning air was cool and slightly damp with fog. He'd failed her. If he'd only had the sense to reveal his identity, he could have forced Mr. Hudson's hand.

He stopped and glanced back in the direction of the publishing office. Maybe he ought to return and do precisely that.

No. Blackmail was not the honorable way to handle matters.

Certainly not when dealing with someone like Mr. Hudson. The man was only doing what he needed for the sake of his business. Threatening him would be wrong.

Expelling a weary breath, Brody resumed walking. He reached the next corner and prepared to cross when he heard Anthony calling to him.

"You're out early," Anthony said as he drew his horse close to where Brody stood.

"As are you."

Anthony grinned. "I often go for a ride before breaking my fast. It's a marvelous way to start the day."

"As is a brawl, I'd imagine." When Anthony gave him a puzzled look, Brody told him, "I've a good mind to pull you off that horse and give you a sound thrashing."

Anthony's grin faded. "Whatever for?"

"Don't pretend you don't know." When Anthony merely stared at him, Brody threw his arms up in exasperation. "You knew she wasn't a man and you bloody well should have told me as much."

"Ah."

"Exactly so," Brody muttered. He crossed his arms and glared at his friend. "What a laugh you and your wife must have had at my expense."

"You're wrong there, Brody." Anthony's voice was soft but grave. "Harriet's secret was not ours to tell, but I must confess I hoped you'd find out if you spent additional time with her. It was clear to me that the two of you got along – that you cared for her and that—"

"We are *not* getting into what all of this led to."

"Hold on." Anthony's eyes brightened. "You're not suggesting you... Good lord, did you make a move on her while you still thought she was Harry?"

"As I said, we are *not*—"

Anthony howled with laughter. "Oh lord. You've given me an excellent idea for our next novel."

"I'll kill you." Brody grabbed hold of Anthony's leg. With one quick yank, he'd hauled him to the ground.

Anthony landed in a heap, still sputtering with mirth as he pulled himself upright. "A roguish duke persuaded to give up the fairer sex in favor of—"

Brody's fist connected with Anthony's jaw, sending him back into a sprawl. He frowned and rubbed at the spot where he'd taken the hit. "I suppose I deserved that. Help me up, will you?"

"I made an arse of myself. The fact that Harriet's

being a woman makes everything so much simpler is completely beside the point."

"I can't believe you never suspected." Anthony stood, holding the reins while his horse pushed its muzzle against his shoulder.

"No one did." Brody snorted. "Her disguise was very effective."

"Only because you allowed it to be. Admit it, now that you know, it's obvious she's not male."

Brody had to agree this was true. If one took the time to truly study Harriet's features, there was no denying that her facial structure was most assuredly feminine. His only comfort was knowing he wasn't the only one she'd fooled. None of her colleagues had any idea.

He nodded, then added, "I've got to get going. Finn will be back from his duel soon, and I want to check on Harriet too. She's staying with me and—"

"At your house?" Anthony's eyes looked ready to pop from his head.

"She's sick with the same thing her sister had. I'm caring for her."

"As Harry?"

"Of course. I didn't even realize she was Harriet until after she was…" Brody scratched the back of his neck. "It's not important. But yes, my servants also believe she's a man."

Anthony swung into the saddle. His gaze was serious as it met Brody's. "Be sure to keep it that way if you plan to protect her reputation. She'll be outed as a charlatan otherwise and possibly labeled a whore for living with two unmarried men."

"I know. I'll be careful."

"Please do so or Ada will have my head. She did not support my insisting you go after Harriet yesterday. For precisely this reason."

"Your wife's a wise woman," Brody said, "but I have to confess that I'm glad you did what you did."

"Then why the hell did you punch me?"

"A matter of principal. You understand."

Anthony chuckled, shook his head, and urged his horse into a trot, allowing Brody to head home. He arrived at his house just as a carriage pulled up. The door opened and Finn alit, followed by Rhys.

Brody rushed forward. The amount of relief he felt over seeing his brother alive could not be measured. As much as he'd tried to ignore the danger of dueling, convincing himself that all would be well since Ramsgate had only demanded first blood, Brody had feared for Finn. He'd worried he might provoke Ramsgate into trying to kill him instead.

Thankfully, this was not the case.

"How did it go?" Brody asked, his hand grabbing hold of Finn's upper arm.

"I lost, which is as it should be." Finn angled his jaw to show off the cut he'd received. Splotches of dry blood surrounded the wound. "Lady Fiona's reputation will be preserved. From what I gather, she will be known as the innocent lady the devilish Marquess of Losturn attempted to tarnish. Thankfully, her hero father came to her rescue and no real harm was done."

"And there will be no additional incidents such as this in the future?" Brody asked, his voice firm.

"Correct. I believe I've learned my lesson."

"About bloody time," Brody muttered. He considered his brother and the slightly forlorn look in his eyes. "I realize you think me a hypocrite due to my own history. You believe it unfair that I spent every night out with friends for more than two years, drinking, gambling, and chasing women. And it is, but as your older brother it's my job to guide you and keep you from making the same mistakes I made."

"Mistakes can be educational," Finn said with the barest hint of a smile.

"Agreed, but they can also be ruinous. Pissing away the fortune Papa spent his life protecting is shameful beyond compare. We're both to blame, and while I'll allow that we needed to deal with our grief, destroying what our ancestors built isn't the answer. It has to stop."

"You're right, but I'll need a different distraction then, because losing Papa was…"

Finn's voice cracked and Brody didn't hesitate. He pulled his brother into his arms and held him while he wept. It didn't matter that they were standing on a London pavement for all the world to see. The only thing of importance was being there for Finn.

"How's your guest?" Finn asked with a sniff as they pulled apart seconds later.

"She had a rough night." They entered the house where Rhys, who'd preceded them inside, stood waiting. Brody handed over his hat and gloves and followed Finn up the stairs. "I trust you'll be taking a nap?"

They entered the upstairs hallway. "And you'll be checking up on Miss Michaels?"

A maid exited one of the rooms. She bobbed a quick curtsey and moved toward the servant stairs.

"Despite there being an actual Miss Michaels present," Brody whispered, "it would be prudent of us to refer to Harriet as Mr. Michaels as long as she's here."

"Understood." Finn stopped in front of his bedchamber door while Brody continued toward Harriet's. "I'll see you later. If you can, you ought to get some rest too. Your eyes are bloodshot."

Brody sent his brother a backward wave and heard his door open and close. Having reached Harriet's room, he gave the door a gentle rap. A faint response from within urged him to ease the door open. He glanced toward the bed where Harriet sat, propped against her pillows, and entered.

"I'm glad you're awake." He closed the door and shifted his gaze to the bedside table. A plate containing a half-eaten piece of toast sat there. "Looks like you managed to get some food down."

She gave him a weak smile. "I tried."

"Have you been awake long?" he asked, removing his jacket while approaching the bed.

"Just half an hour or so."

When he reached her, he pressed his palm to her forehead and felt his heart slow to a steadier rhythm. "You're not as hot as before. I believe your fever's decreasing."

"My eyes are still warm and incredibly heavy. It hurts to keep them open."

"Then close them and try to sleep a bit more. I'm sure you must be exhausted after what you've been through."

"I am." She'd closed her eyes as he suggested and pulled her covers up higher. Brody helped arrange them. He then checked the bucket and chamber pot to see if either needed cleaning.

"There's nothing quite like the handsomest man you know looking to see if you've got some more vomit available for his perusal." Harriet groaned.

"Your eyes are supposed to be closed," he chastised then sent her a broad smile. So he was the handsomest man she knew? He rather liked that, he decided, puffing out his chest a bit more.

She snorted. "I almost hope this is contagious, so I can give you the same kind of treatment."

"The wonderful kind where I climb into bed and hold you against me?" He was already kicking his shoes off and shucking his jacket.

"I'll admit that was rather lovely." She hesitated briefly before saying, "I missed you when I woke and you weren't there."

"I'm sorry." He climbed into the bed and drew her back up against his chest. "There was something I had to take care of. I'll tell you about it later."

For now, all he wanted was for them both to get the rest they needed. So he wound one arm around her and searched for her hand, then laced their fingers together and pressed a kiss to the nape of her neck.

"Sleep well," she murmured, her words quickly fading.

"You too." He squeezed her hand for good measure and gave himself over to sleep.

When he woke once more, it was not to the gentle calm of the woman he loved being right there beside him, but rather to the sort of gasp every man feared – the kind that warned of an ensuing scandal.

It was followed by a horrified, "Praise the lord and all his apostles, my master's a bugger!"

CHAPTER TWENTY-ONE

Harriet shot upright the moment she heard the stricken words. She stared at the maid who stood inside the doorway, her eyes wide with dismay.

"Betsy," said Brody. Having woken as well, he was already sitting up in bed. "It's not what it looks like."

Betsy shook her head. "Ho…How can it not be?"

This was a very good question, Harriet decided. After all, the maid believed her to be a man. And Betsy had not only walked in on Harriet and Brody in the same bed. The bedding had also been partially tossed to one side and Harriet's nightgown pushed all the way up to the top of her thigh. Worse, they'd been sandwiched together when Betsy arrived, with Brody's arm snuggly around Harriet's waist.

Not good.

"I can explain," Brody told her. "If you'll please close the door."

"And risk getting locked up in here with two perverts?" She clucked her tongue. "Not on my life, I tell you. I'm a God-fearing woman, Your Grace, and what you're about is a hanging offense. I'll not be a party to it."

"You don't understand, Betsy. I'm not…" He stared at the maid while she stared back. "Mr. Michaels isn't…I mean, we weren't…Just give me a chance to clarify things."

Betsy shook her head wildly. "I'm sorry. I've always liked and respected you, which is why I'll not mention a word of this to another soul. That said, this is too much. You give me no choice but to seek work elsewhere."

"Please…" Brody tried, his expression twisted with pain.

Harriet's heart ached for him. All of this was her fault. She could not allow this woman to threaten his life and his reputation, as Harriet knew she'd likely do, despite her words to the contrary. Containing this sort of information would be a struggle. She'd let it slip at some point and then the world would believe that Betsy found the Duke of Corwin in bed with his male lover.

The rest of Brody's servants would verify that Mr. Michaels had indeed been a guest at that time.

She couldn't allow for any of that to happen. Not after all Brody had done for her.

"Betsy," she tried, adding as much strength as she could to her weak voice. "The duke is correct. You've mistaken the situation."

"I applaud your attempt at trying to muddle my mind, but I know what I saw, Mr. Michaels. You in his arms, intertwined like a pair of lovers."

"You're right," said Harriet. She swung her legs over the side of the bed and took a deep breath.

"You don't have to do this," Brody informed her while giving her shoulder a gentle touch of his hand.

"Of course I do. It's the only way to stop this mess I've created from hurting you further." She planted her feet on the floor and pushed herself upright, using the edge of the bed to hold herself steady. "My name is not Mr. Michaels."

Betsy snorted. "Your name hardly signifies, sir. It's your gender that's the problem."

"Agreed. Which is why you should also know that I'm not the man you believe me to be. I'm a woman."

Betsy's jaw dropped. She gaped at Harriet for a second before collecting herself and saying, "I don't believe you. If you were a woman I'd have noticed. Everyone would have."

"Look closer," Harriet told her. "I swear to you upon the soul of my mother that I am in earnest."

Betsy firmed her mouth and gave Harriet a dubious look before glancing at Brody.

"Go ahead," he encouraged.

Looking much like she was about to get burned, Betsy stepped nearer and peered at Harriet's face. "I'm sorry, but you could be either or as far as I'm concerned."

Brody, who'd also gotten out of bed, sighed with what sounded like pure frustration. "She's a woman, Betsy. I assure you."

"And I think you're both trying to trick me in order to save your hides."

"Betsy, you've seen me with countless women before," Brody argued. "I had a mistress for years."

Not something Harriet cared to envision. An ugly emotion twisted inside her, attempting to clutch at her heart.

"True," Betsy agreed, "but maybe that was the ruse, to prevent the world from figuring out what your true nature really is."

"Oh, for the love of all that's holy," Harriet hissed as she pulled up her nightgown. "There. Do you believe me now?"

"Um…" Betsy backed away a few steps. She glanced at Brody, who was presently pinching the bridge of his nose while muttering something incoherent. Betsy's gaze returned to Harriet. "How… I mean why…"

"I did it for work-related reasons," Harriet explained. She pulled her nightgown back down.

"I see." Betsy frowned. "So you're to be his new mistress?"

"No," Brody said, his voice clipped.

Betsy blinked. "I don't understand. What else can she be?"

"I'm merely a friend," Harriet tried. "His Grace was kind enough to help me and my sister, that's all."

"And it looks like you gave what he asked for in return," Betsy remarked. "There's a name for that, you know."

"Don't," Brody warned.

"It's called whoring, my dear."

"Get out," Brody told her before raising his voice to a roar. "Get out of my house this instant!"

Betsy stumbled backward. "You're mad. And to think I had such high respect for your poor parents."

"How dare you bring them into this?" Brody asked.

Betsy retreated to the hallway. "They'd be ashamed of how low you've fallen."

"Pack your things," Brody seethed as he crossed to where Betsy still stood, "and leave. I want you gone within the hour."

"You needn't worry yourself about that," Betsy told him. She raised her chin as though with defiance. "No way I'm staying here for one second longer than what I have to."

Brody slammed the door in her face and promptly punched the wall. "Damn!"

"So much for keeping a low profile," Harriet muttered. She bit her lip as the magnitude of their actions came tumbling down around her.

She might have proved she wasn't a man and saved Brody from charges of sodomy. But she'd ruined her alter ego. Harry had been destroyed. He couldn't exist when the truth was out there, ready to spread at this very second. It would only be a matter of time before Mr. Hudson found out about it. Such things would make their way to the gossip columns. Especially when a duke was involved. And now that Betsy required work, she'd probably sell the story the first chance she got.

To suppose it might be bottled up would be naïve.

"Why did you do that?" Brody demanded.

He was glaring at her from across the room, looking strangely feral but also wildly appealing. Her brain was clearly affected by the lingering effects of her fever. She wasn't thinking clearly or she would have known to be very afraid of that angry gleam in his eyes.

Oddly enough, she was anything but.

"I couldn't let her think you were intimately involved with a man. She'd have called the authorities on you."

"I am a duke, Harriet. I'm fairly sure I could have discredited her somehow."

"So you would have lied?"

"Of course not." He was prowling toward her with menacing strides. "I would have told the truth – explained the situation for what it was."

She raised her chin. "How is that different from what I did?"

"It just is." His eyes were aflame when he came to a halt before her, so close she could feel the heat of his body. Breathing raggedly, he traced the side of her face with the back of his hand. When he spoke next, his voice had softened to barely a whisper. "You gave up everything for me."

"And I would do it again, Brody."

He held her gaze. "Why?"

Ignoring the pounding of her heart and the uncomfortable queasiness settling deep in her stomach, she told him all he needed to know. "Because I love you."

His answering kiss was instant, unapologetic, and fierce. He kissed her as though he were starved, as if he'd been parched for a thousand years, like she was the essence of life itself – the key to his survival. It was rough and needy. His hands were everywhere, clutching and gripping, his fingertips pressing into her flesh and holding her to him.

"I'm sorry," he gasped as he broke the kiss and buried his face in the crook of her shoulder. Breathing hard, he managed to ask, "Are you all right?"

She chuckled lightly. "I was pretty dizzy before.

Now I'm—"

"God, I'm a beast." He loosened his hold and eased her onto the edge of the bed. "Sorry, but how could I not respond as I did after what you just told me?"

She tried not to think of the fact that he hadn't repeated the words. It wasn't important.

Unable to speak past the sudden lump in her throat, she merely nodded.

"We will get through this. Betsy will not destroy your reputation, Harriet. I'll save you as you saved me."

"It's too late for that, I should think. She'll say what she will and the gossip will spread."

"Most likely," he agreed. "You will be sneered at as a result, your sister ruined by association."

"Yes," she whispered as tears filled her eyes. She'd sacrificed not only herself, but Lucy as well. What sort of sister did that?

"Unless you're beyond reproach," Brody murmured. He leaned his forehead against hers and said, "Marry me, Harriet."

She blinked. "What?"

"If you're my wife and duchess, all of this goes away."

"Brody, I don't think—"

"No one will dare say a word against you. I swear it."

"It's very heroic of you to offer, but..." She shook

her head.

"Think of Lucy." His intense blue eyes bored into hers. "She'll have a chance at the future your parents wanted for her, and while I'll admit I lack the funds one might expect of a duke, I plan to do better. All I'm asking is for you to give me a chance."

A chance at forever. A marriage from which there could be no escape if either of them changed their mind. She wasn't so worried about herself for she knew what was in her heart. But what about him? He'd made no declaration of love. His only motivation, it seemed, was the chance to be the hero. And where would that leave them as they settled into their daily routine?

For a second, she considered agreeing on the condition that he would swear fidelity to her, but she quickly abandoned that notion. It wouldn't be fair. If he tired of her, he should be permitted to find his happiness elsewhere. This would not be a love match for him, but it would be convenient. For her.

Only a fool would walk away from the chance of a lifetime.

Harriet took a deep breath and expelled it slowly. Marrying a man she loved without knowing if he could ever love her in return would likely kill her, but he'd made the one argument to force her hand. She had to do it for Lucy.

With this in mind, she gave her answer. "Very well. I accept."

CHAPTER TWENTY-TWO

Brody was over the moon. He'd not been this thrilled before in his life. Harriet not only loved him, she would also be his to love and adore until death did them part. Perching on the bed beside her, he drew her gently against him and pressed a kiss to her cheek. He'd been much too forceful before, considering she'd been sick all night and was only now starting to show signs of improvement.

Restraining himself had been near impossible though. But he made the effort while adding additional kisses against the edge or her mouth and across her delicate jaw. A salty flavor filled his mouth and he realized to his dismay that she wept.

"You won't regret this," he promised.

"I know," she whispered, "but what about you?"

Her question forced him to sit back and think.

He stared at her in wonder while pondering her watery eyes. Raising his hand, he swept a stray lock aside and tucked it behind her ear. "I see no reason why I would."

She sniffed a little. "You've known me a very short time, during which you thought I was male. Your acquaintance with Harriet is new, Brody, so I do fear it may lead to some disappointment."

He stiffened and slowly withdrew his hand. "My attraction to Harry was unique. It never would have occurred if you'd actually been a man, which means that it wasn't him. It was you. Obviously, I mean, considering you are one and the same."

"What you thought to be true has still been turned on its head."

"Undoubtedly," he agreed, "but the burning desire I feel for you hasn't lessened. If anything it has increased now that I'm back in familiar waters. Were it not for your being unwell, I'd have you right here this instant."

She gulped and her face turned a bright shade of red. "No one has ever told me such things before."

"I should bloody well hope not," he muttered.

Unable to resist, he set his palm on her knee, then leaned in and nipped at her earlobe. Her answering moan heated his blood like nothing else. No doubt about it. He very much wanted this woman. Knowing he'd have to wait, he settled Harriet into bed and tucked the blankets around her.

"Try to get some more rest, my soon-to-be wife." He kissed her lips, pausing briefly before withdrawing. "There's much for me to attend to. If you're hungry for something more than what's left on your plate, please use the bell pull."

As much as he longed to stay, he forced himself to return downstairs. Rhys would require an explanation regarding Betsy's dismissal. Finn would have to be informed of Brody's upcoming nuptials. A wedding would have to be planned, which meant that his mother…

Brody froze on the stairs.

How the hell could he have forgotten her?

He bolted down the last few steps and ran to his study.

"Everything all right, Your Grace?" asked Rhys. The butler had materialized in the doorway before Brody was able to take his seat.

"Yes. I mean no. Something's come up." Brody stared at Rhys who stared right back, an expectant look in his eyes. "Do come in and I shall explain."

"Very good, Your Grace." Rhys entered the study and closed the door.

"I am to marry," Brody informed him, choosing to get directly to the point.

The tiniest flicker of movement on Rhys' brow betrayed his surprise before he managed to school his features once more. "Felicitations. May I inquire about your choice of bride?"

"It is to be my current houseguest."

Rhys' jaw dropped. "The man upstairs?"

"She's not a man, Rhys. She's a woman pretending to be a man."

"Well I'll be," Rhys muttered. Forgetting himself, he sank to the nearest chair. "Why on earth would she do that?"

"Suffice it to say she had her reasons."

When Rhys just sat there in baffled silence, Brody eventually cleared his throat. Rhys leapt to his feet, straightened his posture, and stared straight ahead. "My apologies, Your Grace. I fear you caught me a bit by surprise."

"Only a bit?" Brody asked with a chuckle. He sobered in response to the grave expression his butler gave him. "In any event, I'll need to inform the duchess and set about planning the wedding."

"If I may, I would suggest that you ask your intended to leave the house until after you're married. Not very proper, having an unmarried lady residing with you and your brother."

"Agreed. She'll depart as soon as she has recovered. Informing Mama will help make this easier. I'd rather Miss Michaels and her sister visit her instead of returning to their former home."

"Duly noted, Your Grace. If you prepare a note for the duchess, I'll make sure it gets delivered."

"Thank you, Rhys." Brody tightened his jaw.

"There's another matter I need to bring to your attention, in case you've not yet been made aware."

"If you're referring to Betsy's departure, then I am already informed."

"I see." Brody considered explaining his reason for sacking the maid, but decided against it. Judging from Rhys' stunned response when Brody had mentioned Harriet's true identity, he'd no idea why Betsy was leaving, and Brody had little desire to rehash the details. Instead he said, "I'll leave it to you to find an appropriate replacement."

"Of course. Is there anything else, Your Grace?"

"Just the note, if you'll wait a moment." Brody dipped his quill in the inkwell and wrote a quick line inviting his mother to tea that same afternoon. After adding his signature to the bottom, he blotted the page, folded it neatly, and sealed it with a crimson blob of wax. "Here you are."

The butler departed and Brody took a deep breath before expelling it slowly. It was done. His mother would be informed. There was no going back now. In all likelihood, everyone between her home and here would know something was afoot before she arrived in his parlor. Why else would he summon her when they'd not spoken in over two years?

Sighing, he removed himself to the dining room where he finally managed to eat a much-appreciated breakfast. Lord, he was hungry. So he put away several slices of toast along with some bacon and eggs.

When he was done, he informed Rhys that he would be stepping out for a couple of hours. For as much as he hoped to give Harriet all the time she needed to plan a proper wedding, he thought it best to have a special license on hand, all things considered.

It was almost noon by the time he returned.

"Is Miss Michaels still sleeping?" he asked Rhys when he handed him his gloves.

"I believe so, but her sister is up. You'll find her in the music room with your brother."

So Finn was awake as well. Perfect. Brody went to find the pair and was rather charmed when he saw them sitting next to each other on the bench in front of the pianoforte.

"It goes like this," Finn said before playing a few notes to a simple tune. "Now you try."

Brody watched as Lucy made the effort, his heart expanding ten-fold when the girl's success led to laughter. Lord, it seemed like forever since music and good cheer had filled this house. Not since his father's death and his mother's decision to relocate.

Everything had gone sideways since then.

He shook his head, banishing the maudlin thought, and gave the doorjamb a couple of knocks to announce his presence.

Finn stood while Lucy waved at him from her spot on the bench.

"How's the patient?" Finn asked. He appeared, it seemed, to try and hide a smirk, only to fail abysmally.

"Better. Thank you for asking. She's resting now." He glanced across at Lucy, whose attention had quickly returned to the keys on the instrument. "How are you fairing today, Lucy?"

She met his gaze. "I'm feeling much better. Perfectly fine, actually. I even managed to eat some eggs along with a bit of bacon."

"I'm pleased to hear it."

"Will Harry be down soon?" she asked. "Losturn says he's also been sick so I didn't want to go check in case I disturbed him."

Brody shared a quick look with Finn before approaching Lucy. "I know Harry's your sister and that her real name is Harriet."

Lucy stilled. Concern puckered her brow. "Oh no. No one's supposed to know that. I hope I didn't say anything to give her away."

"You're not to blame," Brody hastened to tell her. "I found out from Harriet herself."

"I see." Lucy bit her lip. "What will happen now?"

"Well, something did come up – something that put your sister's reputation at risk. Which is why I've asked her to be my wife."

Lucy gasped while Finn voiced his own dismay.

"Harriet will be a duchess?" Lucy asked, her eyes wide.

"Yes," Brody confirmed.

"And she will live here?"

"As will you," Brody told her, intent on putting the girl at ease.

"Cor...that's marvelous news!"

"It's certainly sudden," Finn murmured.

Brody turned to him. "You disapprove?"

"I didn't say that, but are you certain this is what you want?" The look Finn gave him was steady. "Marriage is permanent, Brother."

"I'm aware, and yes, I'm certain. She's...perfect for me."

"Then I shall wish you both happy," Finn said as he pulled Brody into a hug.

Brody patted his brother on the back and stepped back. "I've summoned Mama."

Finn snorted. "You've certainly decided to shake things up around here."

"I'm not the one who engaged in a duel this morning." Brody gave Finn a pointed look.

"A duel?" Lucy asked. "Over a lady?"

"In a manner of speaking," Finn said.

"How positively romantic."

"It really wasn't," Brody told her. "It was mad."

"Says the man who's marrying a woman he thought was a man until just—" Finn glanced at the clock and grinned— "twelve hours ago or less?"

"Precisely." Brody had no idea how he managed to say this with a straight face. In truth, the situation was farcical. Harriet's concern about their brief acquaintance had merit. Had Betsy not threatened to cause a scandal, he never would have proposed. Or rather, he'd have waited. But for what? Harry was Harriet and Harriet was Harry. He'd fallen in love with Harry's smile, the sparkle in his eyes, and his wonderful personality.

None of that would change. Harriet had the same smile, the same sparkle in her eyes, the same wonderful personality he so adored. And after last night, it honestly felt like he'd known her forever. Marrying her would be easy.

Or so he thought.

Until his mother arrived.

CHAPTER TWENTY-THREE

The Duchess of Corwin was uncommonly tall for a woman. At just over six feet in height, she was only slightly shorter than her sons. This, however, did not diminish her elegance. Edwina Evans moved with the grace of someone who weighed no more than the air around her. Even after two years, Brody acknowledged, she hadn't changed.

She arrived in the parlor after being announced, but rather than greet him or Finn, she remained near the door while giving them each a hesitant look. "What's happened?"

"An astounding amount," Finn quipped.

"That's not reassuring," Mama murmured.

Brody sighed. "Please have a seat, Mama. Tea and cake will arrive shortly."

She hesitated briefly before crossing to one of the two vacant armchairs. Finn claimed the other, leaving Brody alone on the sofa. A maid arrived bringing the tea tray. It was carefully placed on the table between everyone. She arranged the cups and saucers, then offered them each a plate for the cake before she bobbed a quick curtsey and left, shutting the door on her way out.

Mama picked up the teapot and started to serve, as she'd always done when they'd lived together. It was the strangest feeling – like visiting a dream from another lifetime.

"I'm to be married," he blurted before she was done pouring. He stood and proceeded to pace the length of the room. It had not been his intention to make the announcement like that. He'd meant to wait for them to exchange a few pleasantries first. But after more than two years of not seeing each other, the words had simply popped out.

He took a breath. What a relief it was to have that off his chest. He glanced at Mama, who'd turned to look at him with a slightly owlish expression.

"Are you really?" she asked.

"Yes."

She suddenly smiled. "What a relief."

He halted his strides. "I beg your pardon?"

"Keeping in mind the urgency of your note, I feared you might have gambled away the estate."

He gaped at her. "How could you possibly think so?"

"You're honestly asking that of me?" She shook

her head. A pained expression captured her features. "I lost him too, you know. What I hadn't expected was also losing my sons."

Brody took a few steps in her direction. Her comment speared him. "You didn't lose us, Mama."

"Didn't I?" The smile she gave him was so sad it twisted his gut. "My words of warning fell on deaf ears. Worse, you told me to leave you alone, that I was to stay out of your affairs. You were duke now and you'd manage things as you saw fit."

"I don't believe those were my exact words," he muttered, recalling all too well how angry he'd been with the world back then. He'd taken it out on everyone, especially those who'd attempted to make him move on, be responsible, stop wallowing in his own grief. Like Mama.

"You're my son," Mama muttered. "But you were intent on destruction, and you pushed me away. Both of you did."

"I know," Brody admitted. "I'm sorry. I—"

"Me too." To his amazement, she stood and gathered him in her arms, hugging him until he felt the world shift. "I shouldn't have stayed away. I should have visited both of you, but as time went on it got harder. More awkward. So I'm glad you finally chose to reach out."

"Do I get a hug as well?" Finn asked.

Mama grinned and let Brody go so she could

embrace Finn next. "I trust your duel went well this morning since you're still breathing?"

"You know about that?" Finn asked in dismay. He stepped out of her arms and gave her a curious look.

She chuckled. "Did you honestly think I wouldn't take steps to ensure I'm informed of what my sons get up to? Which brings me back to you, Brody. I hope you didn't take that job because of financial troubles."

Stumped, Brody lowered himself to the sofa once more and reached for his cup. "Have you been spying on us?"

"Let's not get distracted by details. I was concerned, that's all you need to know."

"Right." He sipped his tea, not the least bit comfortable with the idea of some person his mother had hired sneaking about and taking note of his actions. Shuddering, he told her, "The job was a means to an end, but it does have to do with financial troubles. The fact is, I should have listened to you. I'm sorry I didn't, but regret won't get me anywhere at the moment. On the contrary, it's time to act."

"I think you'd better explain."

Agreeing, he offered Mama a piece of cake before passing the plate to Finn. He then spent the next hour informing his mother what his excessive cavorting and Finn's fondness for gambling had led to. "We're both taking strides to turn our lives around and be the men you and Papa would be proud of, but it's not easy."

She gave him a curious look. "Tell me about this book you've written."

"I'm not the only author involved. Westcliffe and Stratton worked on it too."

"And?"

"It's under contract with Hudson & Co. They expect to print five thousand copies and have it in shops before Christmas. My share of the advance should be delivered before the end of the week."

Her wide smile accentuated the fine lines next to her eyes. "I think that's marvelous news, Brody. Having a project you're fond of can be extremely rewarding. Your father loved his investments and as a result, he got good at making them grow. But it needn't be like that for you. Your purpose in life may be different. What matters is that you've a source of income and that you're content."

"I'm afraid my source of income won't be enough," he murmured. "Which is why I've decided to do as Westcliffe has done and sell off the things I don't need. After that, I'll seek advice on investing – as I should have done in the first place."

"The best lessons in life come from experience. I'm pleased to see that you've both been acquiring some." She ate her cake while Finn promised he'd never play cards again or approach a woman unless he intended to ask her to dance. Mama rolled her eyes but smiled before turning her full attention on Brody. "I'm terribly eager to learn the identity of your intended. Who is she and when do you plan to marry?"

Brody steeled himself. "Her name is Harriet Michaels."

Mama tilted her head. "I don't believe I know of a debutante by that name."

"That's because she's not a debutante, Mama. She's…a wonderful woman I met while working at Hudson & Co."

"Are you saying she's of the working class?" Mama's voice had dropped an octave.

"In a manner of speaking." Seeing the worried look in his mother's eyes, he added, "Her parents were gentry. They lived in Chilham, but when her father died without a will, she and her sister were tossed out onto the street by some awful cousin. Harriet came to London in search of work. She's been supporting her sister these past two years."

Mama slowly nodded. "I applaud her. Being gently bred and then having to pull up one's sleeves and make a living is no small feat. Least of all for a young woman who also has a sister to care for. I think I can see how you'd fall for someone like that."

"So you approve?"

"I'll let you know once I meet her."

"That can be arranged as soon as she wakes." Brody shot a look at Finn, who was pressing his lips so hard together his eyes bulged. He looked on the verge of howling with laughter.

"I beg your pardon?" asked Mama.

"She's upstairs," Brody confessed.

Mama set her palm to her breast and leaned back, a horrified look in her eyes. "Not in your bedchamber, I hope."

"Of course not," Brody hissed. "What do you take me for?"

"Well, the last time I saw you there were three scantily clad women draped over that very sofa." She nodded in his direction.

"Just three?" Finn chuckled.

"Shut up," Brody told him. To his mother he said, "She's in the first guest bedchamber on the left. Her sister was sick, so I invited them both to stay here where they'd be more comfortable, and then Harriet got sick as well. She was up most of the night but was much improved this morning."

Mama stared at him. "She's an unmarried woman, Brody. What on earth were you thinking?"

"That *she* was a *he*?" Finn snickered.

"What?" Mama sputtered.

"It's true," Brody confessed. "Her disguise was very convincing so—"

"Please stop right there." Mama held up her hand. She'd never looked more appalled. "I don't even want to imagine what that's all about. The point is she can't remain here. It wouldn't be right and it certainly wouldn't help you have a wedding devoid of scandal."

"Agreed, which is why I would like for you to invite her to visit."

"With me? At my home?"

"Exactly, Mama."

"But I don't even know her."

"She's your soon-to-be daughter-in-law and the future mother of your grandchildren." He leaned forward. "She's also had a hellish couple of days and could do with a bit of kindness. I trust you can make that happen?"

Mama stared at him in openmouthed amazement before she eventually closed her mouth and gave him a dignified nod. "Of course."

"Thank you." He settled against the sofa and told her, "I've had the presence of mind to procure a special license in ord—"

"Oh no." Mama gave her head a firm shake. "There will be none of that, Brody. Not when I'm finally getting the chance to plan a wedding. My mother planned mine, you know. I've been waiting a good twenty-six years for this moment."

"Really?" Brody glanced at Finn, who looked as shocked as he felt.

"I'll speak with my cook, and yours as well. They can collaborate on the food. Your fiancée and I can have a cake-tasting session. We'll visit the florists – I can think of ten without even trying. And the wedding gown must be ordered. That will be fun, going over fashion plates and picking out the right shade of silk and lace. And the vicar, we mustn't forget about him. I trust St. George's will suit or did you have another church in mind?"

Finn leaned across the table and whispered to Brody, "I think she's gotten used to the idea of Harriet living with her for a while."

Brody nodded. He was astonished to see how excited she was. Beyond that, he was pleased. He'd made peace with his mother, and while he regretted Harriet having to leave his home, there was comfort in knowing that it was a brief but necessary arrangement. Within a month, she'd be his. He'd make certain of it.

CHAPTER TWENTY-FOUR

Harriet was in hell. There was no other way to describe the ordeal Brody's mother was putting her through. It was so exhausting, she almost looked back on the bedridden night she'd spent in his home with longing. At least she'd been able to rest then.

Now her days were spent at the modiste's. She'd been fitted for not just one, two, or even three dresses, but twenty. This was the number of gowns her future mother-in-law insisted on Harriet having at her disposal. Less wouldn't do, not even when Harriet argued that Brody couldn't afford it.

"Don't worry," the duchess said. A sly smirk followed. "I'll pay."

Apparently she had her own funds. She'd also made it clear that Harriet mustn't argue. So she hadn't. Except when the duchess had voiced her disapproval of Harriet's hair and suggested they order a wig. Harriet had drawn the line there but went along with everything else.

After all, despite feeling like an overused doll, she was grateful. Especially when she saw the positive effect the wedding plans had on Lucy. She marveled at everything, from the softness of the dresses ordered for her as well, to the sweetmeats she received one afternoon as a treat, to the music lessons the duchess provided.

Everything was either "brilliant" or "smashing".

Harriet had no cause for regret. Why would she when she was to marry a duke?

In truth, she was thrilled.

At least for the most part.

"I believe I'll go for a walk," she told the duchess one day after breakfast. What she longed for was some time alone, away from all the fuss.

"Where to?" asked the duchess. "Maybe I'll join you."

"Um…" She sent Lucy a frantic look and prayed her sister would come to her rescue in one way or other.

"I was hoping you'd help me with the piece you've been teaching me how to play." Lucy gave the duchess a wide smile. "It's so much easier when you show me than when I practice alone."

"All right." It was clear that she had no desire to disappoint Lucy. Brody's mother was a lovely woman. It was shocking to know that the two hadn't spoken in over two years. She glanced at Harriet. "I'm afraid you'll have to go alone then. Just make sure to take Fiona with you as chaperone."

Harriet agreed and set off with the maid soon after.

"I plan to call on a friend," she said to Fiona as they strolled. "The house isn't far."

They soon arrived at Emily's home where the butler showed them to the library.

"Look up," said the butler when Harriet failed to locate her friend. Emily was standing on a ladder, checking books against a list. Harriet thanked the butler for his assistance and he departed.

"What are you up to?" Harriet asked Emily as she moved toward her.

"Rearranging things to make space for the twenty volumes of the encyclopedia I gave Papa for his birthday."

"The one Ada bound?"

"The very same." Emily grabbed a couple of books and descended the ladder. "You're looking well. It would seem that being engaged to a duke suits you."

Harriet forced a smile. "Perfectly so.

Emily frowned and glanced at Fiona, who'd remained near the doorway. "Why don't you go and enjoy some tea and biscuits downstairs in the kitchen? Miss Michaels will call you when she's ready to leave."

"Of course." The maid bobbed a curtsey and left.

Emily took Harriet's hand and led her to a nearby sofa. "Now tell me the truth. Something's troubling you. What is it? How can I help?"

Harriet wasn't sure where to begin. The last thing she wished was to sound ungrateful.

She took a seat "I…"

"Yes?" Emily pressed as she sat beside her.

Harried sighed and relaxed against the sofa. "It's slightly stifling. I'm accustomed to venturing out on my own, to being productive. But now…"

"Planning a wedding is not as rewarding?"

"I realize it sounds ridiculous. Most working-class women would leap at the chance to switch places with me. And I'm grateful for what I have – for this marvelous opportunity. I'm not unhappy, I simply wish there were more freedom. Emily, I feel like I'm constantly being watched, either by servants or by Brody's mother, who's wonderful by the way. But I honestly need a moment alone."

Emily chuckled. "Why do you think I started the book club, or rented a room in which to host it so none of the members would have to come here? Because I too was in need of escape."

Harriet propped her elbow on the armrest and leaned her head against her hand. "I haven't even seen or heard from Brody since leaving his home on Thursday."

"I'm sure he's busy with his own wedding preparations."

"*Everyone* is. I'm already sick of it and there are still more than two weeks to go before he and I say our vows."

"Harriet?" Emily took her hand and gave it a squeeze. "Are you having second thoughts about marrying him?"

Harriet swallowed. She'd started wondering the very same thing. Were it not for Lucy…

"I fear he's making a terrible mistake out of some misplaced sense of duty." And because of Lucy, she was too much of a coward to stop him.

"Why do you say that?"

"Because he proposed in order to save me from ruin."

"That makes no sense whatsoever."

"How can you say that when you know the particulars pertaining to my relationship with him? You know we were found in bed together and that—"

"You needn't go over it all again," Emily said. "I read the letter you sent me. The detail was noteworthy."

"Then you must surely see that he had no choice. He's only marrying me so my name won't be sullied."

Much to Harriet's surprise, Emily smiled with a

hint of humor. "I truly think you're making an issue of something that's hardly an issue at all."

Harriet stared at her friend. "What are you saying?"

Emily bit her lip. She eyed Harriet carefully before saying, "I hope you don't take this the wrong way, but you're not...*known*. Your presence in Corwin's home would not have been of much interest to anyone."

"I'm an unmarried gentlewoman."

"Who's never been out in Society. That maid could have shouted her gossip from the rooftops, but the truth is, no one would have batted an eyelid."

"But..." Harriet dropped her gaze to her lap. Was Emily right? It was true that she hadn't been introduced to the *ton*. Papa had died before she'd had the chance. And Betsy hadn't known her real name. She'd only known her surname - a fairly common one unlikely to draw attention. She glanced at Emily. "Brody insisted marriage was necessary."

"I would advise you to ask yourself why that might be." When Harriet gave her an expectant look, Emily simply grinned. "Think about it."

"You won't tell me?"

"It's only a suspicion for now so I'd rather not say. Besides, if I'm right, you'll be glad you worked it out on your own."

Harriet gave her head a quick shake and stood. "Very well. I'll heed your advice and give it some thought. In the meantime, I wonder if you might help with something. It's impossible for me to go anywhere or do anything without others hovering over me. It's awful, having been used to roam about by myself for so long."

"Do you want to pretend you're still here while sneaking off elsewhere?"

"Just for an hour or so while I visit Hudson & Co. I've not had a chance to return there, and it's been gnawing at my conscience. The men I worked with were more than colleagues. They were my friends. I'd like to tell them what happened and inform them of the church service in case they'd like to attend."

"Are you certain that's wise? You mustn't forget that they knew you as Harry. Arriving as Harriet could make them angry. Especially if they said things to you that they'd never have said to a woman."

It was one of the many reasons why Brody had gotten upset. Still, she felt an obligation toward Mr. Hudson and Oliver at the very least. It wasn't right to disappear despite knowing Mr. Hudson had actively tried to replace her. Stopping by and personally apologizing to the man who'd been so very good to her was the least she could do.

"I'm aware, but that's a chance I'm willing to take."

"Very well then. As long as you won't be too long."

"I'll be back before you know it."

Harriet hugged her friend and departed through the back garden without Fiona being the wiser. She hurried along the streets, not halting to catch her breath until she arrived at her destination.

There she paused and allowed herself a moment to pluck up her courage. Her hands were clammy and her pulse leapt about like a crazed rabbit. Straightening her spine with sheer determination, she stiffened her resolve and entered Hudson & Co.

The editors sitting nearest the door stared at her in surprise, whether because they recognized her or because they didn't expect a lady's arrival, she'd no idea. She'd not known any of them very well, so it could be the latter.

Her gaze went directly to Mr. Hudson, who sat in his usual spot. He was writing something as she approached and must have caught her movement out of the corner of his eye, for he suddenly looked directly at her. There was a pause, as though his brain required a second to adjust to what he was seeing, and then he took a sharp breath. "Harry?"

She smiled. An anxious laugh followed as she clutched the reticule she'd brought along. "It's actually Harriet."

"But…" He blinked and then he shot to his feet. "How?"

"I'm a woman, Mr. Hudson. Not a boy or a man. I just pretended so I would get hired." She glanced toward the print room door. "I'm sorry I deceived you. I'm also sorry I let you down by getting sick."

"People get sick. It happens. Not really anyone's fault, but that still doesn't mean I could keep the position vacant." He scratched the back of his head while looking her up and down. "I can't believe I didn't see it."

Brody had wondered the same, Harriet mused. As had Oliver. "People see what they expect, I suppose. It's what I was counting on when I chose the disguise."

"I'm still rather stumped."

"You're not angry with me?"

"Not really. I mean, I suppose you did lie, but had you not done so I probably wouldn't have hired you. And that would have been my loss, Harr…err…Miss Michaels. You're the finest compositor I've ever had. The new bloke I hired can't hold a candle to your skill and speed. Oliver's beside himself with annoyance."

"I'm sorry to hear it."

"Honestly, I don't see how we'll ever get that blasted book printed on time when he keeps making mistakes." Mr. Hudson eyed her with a shrewd look. "I don't suppose…"

"What?"

"Nah…" He waved his hand dismissively. "Forget it. It was merely a thought. A foolish one at that."

"I'd still like to hear it," Harriet said.

He smiled broadly. "I was only going to ask if you'd like to come back, but judging from the way you're dressed, I daresay your luck has changed and you no longer need the earnings."

"I'm to marry," she informed him. "Mr. Evans has made me an offer and I have accepted."

Mr. Hudson whistled and rocked back on his heels. "Has he now?"

"We'd love for you to attend the service if you're able. It will be at St. George's. Two weeks from this coming Saturday, ten o'clock."

"I'll be there." He pursed his lips. "You should know that Mr. Evans did what he could to convince me to keep you on. I'm sorry to say that I just couldn't risk it. I—"

The print room door opened and Oliver appeared. "Apologies for the interruption, Mr. Hudson, but…Harriet?"

Mr. Hudson glanced between them. "You knew of her disguise?"

"I, um…" A deep shade of red tainted Oliver's cheeks. "I found out by chance."

"On account of something I said," Harriet hastened to add. "A silly mistake."

"Right." Mr. Hudson nodded in Oliver's direction. "What did you wish to tell me?"

Oliver blinked. "Oh. Just that George got angry when I insisted he try and work faster. Words were spoken and he left."

"He left?"

"I realize I probably shouldn't have called him an imbecile. I take the blame for that. But honestly, Mr. Hudson, considering all the mistakes he's made, we'd have been better off if I both read and placed the sorts. Would have taken the same amount of time, but at least it would have been accurate."

Mr. Hudson muttered a curse. "Do that for now and I'll try to find a solution."

"I can help for a bit," Harriet offered. "I've got about fifteen minutes, give or take. Should be enough for at least one page."

"Brilliant." Oliver beamed. "Please let her do it, Mr. Hudson."

"Of course, I'll let her do it," Mr. Hudson said. "I'm keen on success, not failure. But what about Mr. Evans? What will he say to this?"

"Mr. Evans?" Oliver asked.

"My fiancé," Harriet explained.

Oliver grinned. "Congratulations, Harriet. That's smashing news. When's the big day?"

"Two weeks from Saturday, ten o'clock at St. George's. You're invited to attend."

"And I'll be welcome? Looking like this?" He sent her a toothy grin.

She chuckled. "It wouldn't hurt for you to wash and put on a set of clean clothes for the occasion. Now, if you want my help, we'd best get started. I've got to go soon."

"It's bloody good to have you back," Oliver told her as he led the way to the print room where James and Matthew were adding paper to the press. "Look who's here!"

"A woman?" James asked.

"No, you nitwit. It's Harry, otherwise known as Miss Harriet Michaels."

"You're having us on," Matthew said in open dismay.

James stared her up and down. "The face is the same. I actually think it is Harry."

"Except she's not really Harry but Harri*et*. A woman," Oliver said as though he himself had transformed her with a magical trick.

Matthew frowned. "You must have thought we were daft."

"Not at all," said Harriet. "You saw what I intended for you to see. No one knew."

"We talked about stuff we'd never have mentioned to you, had we known." Much like Brody, James looked both angry and hurt. "Good lord, we gave you pointers on how to bed women."

"I realize that, and I'm sorry. If it helps in any way, I didn't mind. On the contrary, I enjoyed the camaraderie I found in your company. You made me feel like I was part of the group."

"Because we thought you were one of us," James insisted. "Only you weren't. You were an imposter pretending to be something you're not. A spy for the other side."

"What?"

"Let's focus on what's important," Oliver interrupted. "George is rubbish but Harriet's here, willing to lend a hand for a spell. Can we please take advantage of that before she's got to be on her way?"

"Fine," James grumbled. Turning, he gave her his back and proceeded to fit the printing frame with a new sheet of paper.

She glanced at Matthew but he only shook his head and went to help James. Maybe coming back had been a mistake. Trudging across the floor, she returned to her familiar spot. She surveyed the table and all of the drawers containing the sorts while Oliver perched on the stool beside her.

"Ready?" she asked.

"Ready," Oliver confirmed.

He proceeded to read while she set the type, her movements as swift and precise as always. The first compositing stick was placed in the form, then the next and the one after that. Harriet crafted the frame around the sticks then began filling the empty spaces between them and the edge of the form with pieces of wood so they wouldn't budge.

The door to the print room swung open before she'd finished. She glanced up and instantly froze as her gaze collided with Brody's.

He did not look the least bit pleased, but there

was little she could do about that at the moment. She bowed her head and continued working. "We're almost done. If you'll—"

"Everyone out." His voice was dangerously low. "I need to speak with Miss Michaels. Alone."

"Can't you—"

"Now," Brody insisted, cutting James off.

Oliver crossed his arms. "You don't work here anymore, Mr. Evans. You've no authority over us."

Brody's jaw tightened. "Perhaps not. But I am the Duke of Corwin, and as such, I'm asking you to let me speak with my future wife in private."

Harriet stared at Brody. She'd not expected him to use his title as leverage, but it seemed to be working. She stiffened as James, Matthew, and even Oliver filed from the room. The door closed and Harriet forced herself to face the man who promised her everything with one exception.

Love wasn't part of the bargain.

"What the bloody hell, Harriet?" Brody fumed before she managed to say anything. He waved his hand and she saw that he held a bouquet of pink roses. "You forced me to scold my mother's maid for letting you give her the slip. And don't even get me started on Lady Emily, your co-conspirator."

"You mustn't blame either. It wasn't their fault."

He stared at her, his expression baffled. "Why would you run off like that?"

"Because I wanted to go for a walk. By myself. As I've been accustomed to doing for quite some time."

"It isn't safe, Harriet. In Mayfair it might be but not in this part of the city." He swallowed hard and she saw that he was not so much angry as he was distressed. "You were attacked not too far from here, or have you forgotten?"

"That was—"

"By thugs who thought you were male. I dare not even imagine what such men would do to a beautiful woman." The compliment made her a little dizzy. She'd known he found her attractive – irresistibly so – but to hear him say it was rather lovely. He shook his head. "If you wanted to come here I would have gladly provided the escort."

"I thought you were too busy." When he gave her a blank look she said, "I've not seen as much as your shadow since leaving your home five days ago, Brody."

"I've been busy tending to my ledgers, correspondence, and selling off items I don't need so we can be comfortable. It's important to me that you have your own maid as well as a horse to ride, should that strike your fancy."

Her heart melted and she reached for his hand. "I don't need any of that."

"You'll be the Duchess of Corwin. Anything less would be unacceptable."

She sighed. "You know, we don't *have* to marry."

"What?" The word was so tightly spoken it sounded as though it might crack.

"I believe this wedding is proving a huge inconvenience to you."

"It's nothing I can't handle."

How positively unromantic. She averted her gaze and fiddled with her skirt while trying to hide the pain in her heart. This marriage would happen for practical reasons alone, and while she'd initially thought she had the strength to go through with it, further reflection had made her realize she didn't. She couldn't marry a man she loved unless he loved her in return.

Oh, Lucy. I pray you forgive me.

"As much as I appreciate your willingness to save me from ruin, I've realized it's not at all necessary."

"Not necessary," he sputtered. "But, Harriet, we discussed this. Betsy saw us together. In bed and with your nightgown almost up to your waist. Of course we have to marry."

"I disagree. A scandal would only occur if I were a noteworthy person. But I'm not, so no one will care."

"*I* will." His sharply spoken remark snapped her gaze back to his. Blue eyes, brimming with some sort of furious passion, pinned her. He tossed the bouquet of roses aside, scattering petals all over the floor, then grabbed her by the shoulders. "You told me you love me. Or was that also a lie?"

"Of course not." How could he think so?

Incomprehension burned in his eyes as he bowed his head and leaned in, bringing his face within one inch of hers. "Then what's the problem?"

"It's that…" She shook her head. He would not make her say it.

"This makes no sense." He retreated a step. "Is this about my disapproval of your coming here unescorted?"

"No."

He studied her before asking, "Do you want to continue working. Is that it? When I arrived, Mr. Hudson asked if such an arrangement might be possible, and I assured him that I would discuss it with you. Of course, you would have to accept the *ton's* disapproval, but as duchess, I'm confident you'll manage."

How could she not love him? "Your generosity means more to me than you can imagine."

"All I want is to make you happy."

"I know, but I don't think marrying me will achieve that."

"Why not?" The look he gave her was one of outrage and, she realized a second too late, unvarnished anguish. He looked like a puppy she'd kicked in the stomach. "If you love me as you claim, then why don't you want to spend the rest of your life with me as much as I want to spend the rest of my life with you? It's all I've been thinking of since we last parted – the joy I will find in loving you with every beat of my heart, but you're…you're crushing me, Harriet, and I don't understand why."

"Oh, Brody." The anguish in his voice was too much. She flung her arms around his neck and hugged him to her, holding him close with all her might. "I didn't realize. Forgive me. I thought your only motivation for marriage was duty."

"But I told you how I felt." He broke away from her and searched her face. "Didn't I?"

She shook her head. "You showed me through actions, not words. But I was blinded by the hurt I felt when I told you I loved you and you didn't say it back. It stopped me from paying attention to what truly mattered."

"Then let me be perfectly clear with you, Harriet Michaels." He pulled her into his arms and nudged her chin with his hand, tilting her head back until their eyes met. "I love you. Desperately. More than I ever believed I would love another soul."

"I love you too," she managed, right before he crushed her mouth with his in a searing kiss that threatened to set her on fire.

CHAPTER TWENTY-FIVE

S tanding in the middle of the bedchamber she
would be sharing with Brody from this day on,
Harriet watched her husband pour two glasses of
port. The wedding had been a lovely affair. She'd
been thrilled to see all her friends from Hudson &
Co. at the church. Mr. Hudson had even handed her
a gift before she and Brody stepped into their
awaiting carriage. It was a beautiful print containing
the date, time, and place of their wedding, beneath
which all of her colleagues had posted a message.

"Did the day meet your expectations?" Brody
asked as he handed her one of the glasses.

"I think it exceeded them." She clinked her glass
against his before taking a sip. "Your mother is an
incredible planner."

He chuckled and took a drink. "I know she exas-
perated you at times."

"Perhaps a little," Harriet agreed. "But it also made her very happy, and you have to admit it was all rather perfect."

"It's not over yet," he murmured, his voice dipping as he traced her shoulder and arm with his fingers. Flames slowly ignited within the depth of his piercing blue gaze as he took a step closer. "The best part's yet to come."

"Oh?" was all she could manage, and even then it was barely more than a whisper.

"Finish your port, Harriet." He caught her gaze while raising his glass to his lips, and held it as they both drank. The air between them, so calm a few moments before, now crackled with anticipation. He collected her glass and set it aside along with his own. "Nervous?"

"Somewhat."

Tilting his head, he appeared to give that some thought. A wolfish gleam appeared in his eyes. He caught her hand and led her across the room until they reached a wall. Nudging her backward, he pressed her against it, then leaned in and brushed his lips against hers.

"Close your eyes," he whispered while kissing his way along the edge of her jaw, "and pretend we're back in the library, picking up where we left off. You weren't nervous then."

"I wasn't myself."

"Not true." His hands gripped her waist, his

thumbs stroking her sides while his teeth nipped her earlobe. "You're the same uninhibited person as you were then."

"Brody…"

His hand slid upward, slowly exploring while she melted against the wall behind her. She sagged in response to his touch and sucked in a breath when his thumb swept inside her bodice. "By tomorrow, I will have tasted you everywhere, Harriet. I'll have kissed you here…here…and finally here."

She gasped at the shocking suggestion. "You can't possibly—"

"Trust me," he purred. "I'll have you so desperate with need that you'll beg me."

Not in a million years, she decided, only to have that thought flitter away as he captured her mouth with possessive force. His hands swept over her curves, mapping each one with a sensual caress. She arched, pressing against him with increasing need. Her fingers caught his cravat, untying it while he undid the back of her gown.

Something ripped and Brody chuckled. "Sorry, my love. I fear I've torn your sleeve."

"It's fine." She was suddenly desperate to rid them both of their clothes. The faster the better. She went to work on his jacket and waistcoat next, pushing and shoving fabric aside until she was able to pull his shirt free and seek the reward she was after.

Her hand swept under the linen and she slowed her movements while meeting his gaze. He paused in the process of pushing her gown up over her head. His breaths came hard and his eyes had darkened to midnight blue.

Holding his gaze, she trailed her fingertips over his stomach.

He hissed and then his eyes flashed with desire.

Emboldened, she dipped her fingertips inside his waistband.

His grip on her gown tightened and when he spoke, his voice was strangled. "Harriet…"

"I want to taste you everywhere too."

His eyes widened, and then he pounced. Her gown disappeared with a few rough tugs before she was lifted into his arms. She landed on the bed soon after. Frayed remnants of lace and silk swirled around her like morning mist. And at the center of it all, stood Brody, watching her with roguish delight.

This was to be their first night together, and Brody intended to make sure his wife enjoyed it so much she'd want to repeat it every night after. So far so good. He smirked, enjoying the flush in her cheeks as she watched him from the bed. She still wore her chemise and stockings, but they would be gone soon enough.

Impatient, he pulled off his shirt and kicked off his shoes.

"Incredible," she murmured, her gaze darting over his torso. "I never believed…that is to say…I always thought the statues were embellished examples of what mortal men aspired toward. Not something they might achieve. But that's not true. You're equally stunning."

If he puffed out his chest any more he'd probably fall on his face. God help him, she certainly knew how to make him feel ten feet tall. He grinned like an idiot, his attempt at playing the devilish seducer momentarily forgotten.

"I'm glad you approve." He unfastened the fall of his trousers and removed the garment along with his smalls and hose. When he straightened, Harriet looked like she might swoon.

"Forget the statues." She gulped. "I've never seen anything more impressive than you."

"And I've never seen a woman more tempting." He climbed on the bed and slid his hand up the length of her leg, gathering her chemise. "Let me help you with this."

The item was slowly removed between kisses, until she too was undressed. He tossed the chemise aside and let his gaze roam, observing each peak and valley of her perfection. Her body was slim and lithe, so gracefully built she moved with what looked like no effort at all.

"I love you," he whispered while spreading his fingers across her hip. He made sure to tell her every day now so she'd have no doubts about his affection.

"And I love you," she told him, her eyes so vibrant and her smile so tender, his heart sparked with joy.

He moved his hand to her thigh as he leaned in and kissed her once more, pressing his mouth to hers, imparting the wonder he felt in this moment. With gentle caresses and soft, soothing touches, he coaxed her toward a state of pure bliss.

"Brody," she gasped, clutching the bedsheets with one hand, his hair with the other.

"I'm right here with you, my love." He positioned himself between her thighs. "Are you ready for more?"

"Yes."

Her arms came around his neck, bringing his mouth to hers in a soul-searing kiss that conveyed one truth as he joined his body with hers. This was where he belonged. With her heart beating against his own. At last.

CHAPTER TWENTY-SIX

Lady Emily Brooke was enjoying her evening enormously. How could she not when two of her dearest friends were finally able to attend a Society ball with her?

She turned to them, the newly minted duchesses of Westcliffe and Corwin. Both had danced excessively with their husbands and were now enjoying refreshments with her. Standing on a balcony above the ballroom, they sipped champagne while watching the revelry below.

"I've never seen so many spectacular gowns," Harriet said, her voice filled with awe. "Or jewels."

"It's quite impressive," Ada agreed. She eyed Emily. "There's something I've been meaning to ask you."

Intrigued, Emily nodded. "Go on."

"It relates to a novel that's due for publication toward the end of October. I'd like for The Lady Librarian to review it."

Emily blinked. Only a few select people knew of her alter ego, and they rarely brought it up in conversation. Ada's decision to do so suggested this book was important to her. Which had to mean… "Who's the author? You or your husband?"

"Um…" The unease that filled Ada's eyes spoke volumes.

Emily smiled. "Don't worry. You needn't tell me. I simply can't wait to read it."

Ada cleared her throat. "It's a romance involving an earl and an innkeeper's daughter."

"Scandalous," Emily said with a grin.

"The book will be published anonymously," Ada muttered.

"Of course. That does make a great deal of sense." Excited on her friend's behalf, Emily said, "Writing a book is no small feat. Acquiring a contract is downright impressive. Please have a copy delivered to me as soon as you're able, and I shall make sure The Lady Librarian writes an outstanding review."

"An honest review," Ada said. "No special treatment."

"Of course. I can't afford to ruin The Lady Librarian's reputation. But, I'm fairly certain the book will be worthy of praise."

"Thank you."

"Any time."

Emily smiled. As a self-proclaimed bluestocking, she centered her life around reading. Her book club, which had begun as a hobby, had turned into a monthly meeting accessible only by invitation. In between these meetings, Emily read and wrote reviews, which appeared in *The Mayfair Chronicle* every Sunday. Over the course of the past two years, The Lady Librarian's fame had increased. A review written by her determined how well a book sold.

"They're bringing more food," Harriet observed. "Shall we return downstairs?"

"Oh yes," Ada said, leaning over the railing. "That does look good."

Emily grinned. She delighted in the excitement with which her friends approached everything she'd been accustomed to all her life. "Let's go."

They descended the stairs and joined the crowd milling about.

Emily grabbed Ada's arm and drew her close to her side. "I'm going to visit the ladies' retiring room first. I'll meet you and Harriet in the ballroom immediately after."

They parted ways, with Ada and Harriet continuing onward, while Emily disappeared through an archway that took her toward the front of the house. After receiving directions from a footman, she turned right and entered a narrow hallway. There she halted when she saw a man striding toward her.

Tall, with thick black hair, intense green eyes, and angular features, he wasn't someone she liked running into for any reason.

Callum Davis, the Duke of Stratton, was best avoided. Unfortunately he reached her before she was able to make her retreat.

"You," she muttered. Not exactly the politest greeting, she admitted, but the annoyance of finding herself in his company was already getting the best of her.

"I could say the same." He raised an eyebrow. "Not very clever, stating the obvious. Although—"

"Did you just call me stupid?"

"Um… No, I don't believe so."

She was fairly certain he had, not that it should surprise her. "Manners have never been your forte, Your Grace. If you'll please excuse me."

She moved with the intention of stepping past him, but he stepped sideways at the same time, blocking her path. "Are you calling my character into question?"

"Um… No, I don't believe so," she said, mimicking his response, even though she generally loathed such childish behavior. But Stratton had the annoying habit of bringing out the worst in her.

His eyebrows dipped. "I ought to challenge you to a duel."

She rolled her eyes. "Knowing you, you'd probably trip and kill me before I got the chance to face you on the field of honor."

"I'm not *that* clumsy." His face had turned a bright shade of red.

"You're right. Forgive me. I didn't mean to suggest that you were."

"I'm fairly sure that's exactly what you intended to do or you wouldn't have said it." Having crossed his arms and firmed his jaw, he glowered at her.

She held his gaze, doing her best to ignore the effect the scolding look in his eyes was having on her. Rather than put her off, it seemed to accentuate his handsome features.

Of course she'd rather die than let him know how attractive she thought him. Besides, looks could only get one so far. Unfortunately, the rest of what Stratton had to offer was not impressive. It also posed a threat to her safety.

She smiled, or at least she attempted to do so while hoping it didn't look like a grimace. "Let's forget this conversation happened. Just permit me to pass and we can both be on our way. Please."

He knit his brow and hesitated for a brief second. Eventually he nodded and stepped aside. But as she moved past, he turned. Too quickly, she'd later reflect. The heel of his shoe caught the hem of her gown, instantly halting her forward motion and sending her into a sprawl.

She landed on her knees, with her hands splayed out in a futile attempt at averting disaster. This was precisely why she wished to avoid the blasted man who presently rushed to her aid. She couldn't go anywhere without him ruining what had begun as a perfectly good day.

Ready for the sequel? *A Duke's Lesson in Charm* is an enemies to lovers romance that I'm sure you'll love!

Order your copy today, and sign up for my newsletter at www.sophiebarnes.com so you don't miss out on my freebies, special deals, and giveaways. You'll receive a complimentary copy of *No Ordinary Duke* with your subscription!

Did you enjoy *A Duke's Introduction to Courtship*? If so, please take a moment to leave a review since this can help other readers discover books they'll love.

Keep turning for my author's note and additional information on A Duke's Lesson in Charm.

Read the final book in the series!

She was the last person he ever expected to marry...

Callum Davis, Duke of Stratton, never expected to get along with Emily Brooke, but thanks to his ward, he starts to realize she's pretty good company. The more time he spends with her, the better he likes her. But rather than let their relationship grow at a gradual pace, a pretend courtship leads to a whirl-wind romance that quickly collapses when Emily finds out what Callum has written about her. Now he must make every effort to prove his love for her is real, or risk losing her forever.

There is only one person Lady Emily Brooke must avoid at all cost, and that's the Duke of Stratton. Since her debut, the man has threatened her safety by stepping upon her toes, spilling drinks on her gown, and sending her head first into a fountain. But when he invites her for a walk so the boy in his care can spend time with her dog, she cannot resist. What surprises her most is how charming the duke can be. Until a mistake on his part makes her question his feelings and his intentions.

BUY NOW!

AUTHOR'S NOTE

Dear Reader,

I hope you've enjoyed the second book in my Gentlemen Authors Series. This time, I delved into early 19th Century printing and the process involved.

Fully understanding how it was done proved a challenge. The articles I found all seemed to have gaps. Either the steps involved weren't fully explained or the tools mentioned lacked the sort of description that made it possible for me to visualize the process from start to finish.

By continuing my search for answers, I finally managed to stitch every piece of information I found together until I was able to get a full picture of what early 19th Century printing actually looked like.

For the purposes of this book, I chose to have

Harriet and her colleagues use the Stanhope Press since this was invented around 1803. It was similar to the Guttenberg Press, but instead of wood it was made of metal and had the capacity for printing around 200 impressions per hour.

Invented in 1814, the Cylinder Press also existed during this period and was used to print the first edition of the *Times*. Capable of printing one thousand-one hundred double sided sheets per hour, it was installed in secret to avoid sabotage from the pressmen who operated the Stanhope Press.

But since Hudson and Co. is a small company, the Stanhope Press seemed like the more reasonable option. Plus, I loved the visual it presented of Harriet's team bustling about, working levers, inserting paper, and adding ink to the type.

But the adventure doesn't end there. *Seductive Scandal* has yet to hit the shelves. Whether or not it will prove as successful as our three heroes hope will be determined in Callum's story. I look forward to sharing his romance with you next in *A Duke's Lesson in Charm*.

Until then, I wish you happy reading.

Sophie

xoxo

ACKNOWLEDGMENTS

I would like to thank the Killion Group for their incredible help with the editing and cover design for this book.

And to my friends and family, thank you for your constant support and for believing in me. I would be lost without you!

ABOUT THE AUTHOR

USA TODAY bestselling author Sophie Barnes is best known for her historical romance novels in which the characters break away from social expectations in their quest for happiness and love. Having written for Avon, an imprint of Harper Collins, her books have been published internationally in eight languages.

With a fondness for travel, Sophie has lived in six countries, on three continents, and speaks English, Danish, French, Spanish, and Romanian with varying degrees of fluency. Ever the romantic, she married the same man three times—in three different countries and in three different dresses.

When she's not busy dreaming up her next swoon worthy romance novel, Sophie enjoys spending time with her family, practicing yoga, baking, gardening, watching romantic comedies and, of course, reading.

You can contact her through her website at www. sophiebarnes.com

For all the latest releases, promotions, and exclusive story updates, subscribe to Sophie Barnes' newsletter today!

And please consider leaving a review for this book.

Every review is greatly appreciated!

Printed in Great Britain
by Amazon